"My name's Sam. And you are?"

"Just leaving," I said with a tight smile. It was for my own good. My friends had told me to make a play for the sandy-haired hunk, but it just wasn't in me to pick up a man in a bar. The girls had bought me a drink for my birthday, given me a ridiculous gift and now it was time to follow their example and head home.

Even though Sam's shiny brown bedroom eyes made the moisture evaporate from my mouth.

He seemed disappointed by my response, but accepting. "Well, nice almost meeting you."

I gathered up my present and had turned to go when he called, "Hey. You forgot something."

I turned back and, to my horror, saw him bending to retrieve the pink sheet of paper containing directions for my present, the "Make Your Own Dildo" kit. The subhead "The Only Set That Lets You Cast It from the Real Thing" seemed to jump off the page. I lunged for the paper, but Sam was too quick. When he lifted his gaze from the sheet, a mischievous smile curved his mouth and his eyes danced. "Looks like fun."

Hmm. On second thought, maybe I *did* have one more birthday present coming to me.

Dear Reader,

It's Harlequin Temptation's twentieth birthday and we're ready to do some celebrating. After all, we're young, we're legal (well, almost) and we're old enough to get into trouble! Who could resist?

We've been publishing outstanding novels for the past twenty years, and there are many more where those came from. Don't miss upcoming books by your favorite authors: Vicki Lewis Thompson, Kate Hoffmann, Kristine Rolofson, Jill Shalvis and Leslie Kelly. And Harlequin Temptation has always offered talented new authors to add to your collection. In the next few months look for stories from some of these exciting new finds: Emily McKay, Tanya Michaels, Cami Dalton and Mara Fox.

To celebrate our birthday, we're bringing back one of our most popular miniseries, Editor's Choice. Whenever we have a book that's new, innovative, *extraordinary*, look for the Editor's Choice flash. And the first one's out this month! In *Cover Me,* talented Stephanie Bond tells the hilarious tale of a native New Yorker who finds herself out of her element and loving it. Written totally in the first person, *Cover Me* is a real treat. And don't miss the rest of this month's irresistible offerings—a naughty Wrong Bed book by Jill Shalvis, another installment of the True Blue Calhouns by Julie Kistler and a delightful Valentine tale by Kate Hoffmann.

So, come be a part of the next generation of Harlequin Temptation. We might be a little wild, but we're having a whole lot of fun. And who knows—some of the thrill might rub off....

Enjoy,

Brenda Chin
Associate Senior Editor
Harlequin Temptation

STEPHANIE BOND

COVER ME

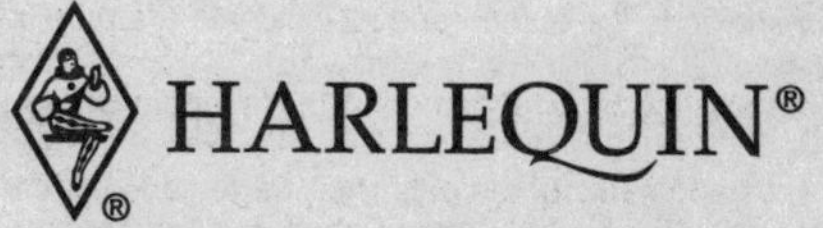

TORONTO • NEW YORK • LONDON
AMSTERDAM • PARIS • SYDNEY • HAMBURG
STOCKHOLM • ATHENS • TOKYO • MILAN • MADRID
PRAGUE • WARSAW • BUDAPEST • AUCKLAND

ISBN 0-373-69164-5

COVER ME

This edition published by arrangement with Harlequin Books S.A.

Visit us at www.eHarlequin.com

Printed in U.S.A.

A NOTE FROM THE AUTHOR...

I love "fish out of water" stories. There's no better way to see the kind of stuff a person is made of than to plunk them into a situation where everything they believe to be true not only can't help them, but sometimes can even get them into more trouble!

Meet Kenzie Mansfield, a label-conscious, career-minded city girl who has to temporarily relocate to a small town to thwart a magazine "cover curse." Kenzie can handle just about anything—or so she thinks!

I hope you enjoy this story, written from Kenzie's point of view as she deals with rural mishaps and tries to maintain a professional distance from the handsome veterinarian she is sent to keep an eye on. Too late, Kenzie realizes this cover assignment might leave her caught between her job and her heart!

Happy reading, and don't forget to tell your friends about the wonderful romantic stories between the pages of Harlequin novels. Visit me at www.stephaniebond.com.

Much love and laughter,

Stephanie Bond

Books by Stephanie Bond

HARLEQUIN TEMPTATION

685—MANHUNTING IN MISSISSIPPI
718—CLUB CUPID
751—ABOUT LAST NIGHT...
769—IT TAKES A REBEL
787—TOO HOT TO SLEEP
805—SEEKING SINGLE MALE

HARLEQUIN BLAZE

2—TWO SEXY!

For Brenda Chin, a fearless editor who keeps raising the bar

1

"I'M ALLERGIC to men," I announced to my three girlfriends between forkfuls of my wickedly garlicky Caesar salad.

Being accustomed to my somewhat obscure proclamations, their vigorous chewing proceeded unchecked. I looked from face to face to see who would cave first. My gaze stopped on Denise and she gave me an eye roll. I could always count on Denise to nibble at my conversation tidbits, however begrudgingly.

"Okay, Kenzie, I'll bite. Are you talking allergic in literal terms, or figurative?"

"Literal," I declared. "I am physically allergic to the male gender."

Cindy squinted. "Like ragweed?"

"Exactly."

Jacki shook her head. "You are hopeless. You're allergic to feathers, mold, pollen, dairy products, rubber and now *men?*"

"Don't forget pet dander," I said.

Jacki pointed with her fork. "Kenzie Mansfield, you are a hypochondriac."

Admittedly, I was. My copy of *Disease and Diagnosis* was as dog-eared as were most women's copies of *Kama Sutra.* At different times in my life, I had been sure I'd had an enlarged spleen, Tourette's syndrome and a brain tumor. Even though those ailments had all been disproved by various and sundry tests, my extensive allergies were documented and real, so I clung to them.

"If I'm a hypochondriac, then you are delusional, Jacki," I said defensively. "You with your theory of choosing men by the *shoes* they wear."

Jacki bristled. "Hey, it worked for me. Ted and I have been going strong for two months. Plus Cindy and Denise have both met guys while testing my shoe theory."

The girls nodded with enthusiasm, and I bit into my lip. I'd missed out on a lot of fun with my friends while working crazy-long hours at *Personality* magazine. They all had boyfriends with nice footwear. I had no boyfriend and seemed to be developing an itch that I suspected was a result of inadvertent contact with our burly Italian waiter.

Jacki gave me a censoring look. "Besides, my theory is simply an extension of human tastes. I never claimed it was scientific—unlike this cockamamie *allergy* hypothesis."

"But me being allergic to men makes perfect sense," I insisted. "Instead of being attracted by male pheromones, my body now goes haywire. My sinus passages close up, my skin gets all blotchy—both of which are medically recognized clinical reactions, by the way."

Jacki was unmoved. "Did you develop this allergy before or after James dumped you?"

My back straightened. "*I* dumped James. But now I think my growing aversion to him was actually the onset of the man allergy."

One of Jacki's eyebrows shot up. "Personally, I think your growing aversion to James was the onset of sanity."

"That, too," I conceded. "But toward the end, I couldn't bear the smell of him, even after a shower." I wrinkled my nose. "And every time he came near me, my neck and chest got all blotchy."

"Do the men you work with give you a reaction?" Denise asked, clearly humoring me, probably to aggravate Jacki.

But I'd given that topic some thought. "No, but most of the men I work with are gay—I don't think they're emitting pheromones directed at me." I pulled a notebook from my purse and flipped through the pages. "For the past two weeks, I've been keeping track of my reaction to all men I come into close contact with—cab drivers, doormen, strangers on the elevator—and it seems that the more *macho* the guy, the more severe my reaction."

Our handsome dark-haired waiter materialized to leave more bread at the table. He winked at me, and I clawed at the instant skin irritation that developed. He hurried away.

"See," I said, extending the white underside of my arms, now red from scratching, as irrefutable proof of my rant.

My friends still seemed dubious.

"So, let me get this straight," Jacki said. "You're allergic to big, strong, alpha men?"

"Exactly." I sank back into my chair, relieved that she finally understood.

Jacki nodded thoughtfully. "There *is* a name for what you're describing."

I did a double take. "There is?"

"It's called being a lesbian."

Denise and Cindy cracked up, but I wasn't amused. I was, however, feeling a little desperate to explain myself. "Don't you see? I'm always attracted to the same type of guy—big and physical—and those relationships have all been disasters. My body has obviously developed this allergy to protect me from my own urges. It's nature's way of telling me that I need to settle down with a nice, quiet, unsexy guy."

The girls looked at me as if I'd grown a second head. If so, I hoped the new head had better hair than the first.

Then Jacki stabbed a chunk of romaine and scoffed. "I think you're freaking out because your birthday is on Thursday and you don't have a man in your life."

My uterus contracted. "That's ridiculous. I'm trying to explain what might be a revolutionary *evolutionary* concept. This development could change the human mating process as the world knows it!"

They stared.

"Besides, I forgot all about my birthday," I lied.

In truth, turning thirty-one loomed more menacingly than any previous anniversary of *moi.* And the only explanation I had for the anxiety was that the year had flamed by so quickly, I was afraid to let it go. Since becoming an assistant to Helena Birch, editor-in-chief of *Personality* magazine, it seemed as if my unremarkable life was slipping through my worked-to-the-bone fingers. A typical day had me leaving my apartment in the dark and arriving home in the dark. If I was lucky, I got to see a sliver of daylight when I delivered towering stacks of reports to Helena's office on the thirteenth floor of the Woolworth Building. (My own office was a closet off a dark hallway.) Today was the first time in eons that I'd had lunch with my friends at our favorite sidewalk café. My indoor arms were ghostly pale next to their sun-kissed limbs, and I had to wear sunglasses against the unfamiliar reflective glare from the sidewalk. My entire body was under assault from the sunshine. And the handsome waiter.

"Well, *we* didn't forget your birthday," Denise said. "We're taking you to Fitzgerald's if you can get away from the office Thursday at five."

I conjured up a smile, already dreading *that* conversation with Helena. My boss was determined to make *Personality* magazine number one in our demographic (young professionals earning over $45,000 per annum who spend a disproportionate amount of income on clothing and cars). Just yesterday we'd learned that we had clawed our way from number nine to number seven in circulation. Good thing, too, because this morning when I'd stared glassily into the mirror brushing my teeth, it had appeared for one brief second as if my eyes were turning nocturnal pink—ergo my spontaneous lunch invitation to my gal pals: my social life simply had to improve. "I'll be at Fitzgerald's," I promised.

Jacki smirked. "Good. But don't forget your antihistamine, Kenzie, just in case you meet a man."

BY THE TIME I had walked back to the Woolworth Building, I had arrived at two conclusions: (1) I felt certain my man allergy would steer me toward a durable guy, and (2) Helena wouldn't fire me if I left early Thursday to celebrate my birthday with friends. Probably not. I'd been working like an android and sleeping with my pager. I had forgone lunches and evenings and weekends. I had turned Helena's desk and schedule into an efficient, well-oiled machine. And maybe my belief that I was indispensable to my boss was more a product of my daylight-deprived mind than it was a reality. After all, equal parts of me were resentful and gleeful that Helena seemed to begin every sentence with the word *Kenziewouldyou.*

I opted for the stairs to extend my lunch hour a wee bit, then realized with a sparkle of alarm that my pager was dead. I trotted up the last two flights, telling myself that nothing dreadful could possibly have happened during my mere sixty-two-minute absence. But when I walked into the lobby of *Personality,* Helena stood in front of a cowering receptionist, flailing her thin arms.

Helena Birch had all the trappings of a superbitch editor-in-chief—she was tall and angular, with laser-blue eyes and a surgical tongue. She was an explosive genius and a social maven, unmarried and unapologetic. I had been duly terrified when I had interviewed for the position of her executive assistant, but strangely enough, we had clicked, and our relationship had grown to resemble what I imagined the bond with my ambitious, strong-willed mother might have been if she were still alive: I lived to please Helena and Helena lived to please no one.

The harried receptionist glanced up and pointed in my direction. "Here's Kenzie now, Ms. Birch."

Helena whirled. "Where have you been?"

I took a deep breath. "Helena, I told you I was going to meet friends for lunch."

Her forehead wrinkled. "You did?"

"Yes."

"Well..." She recovered and crossed her arms over a crisp periwinkle-blue Marie Gray jacket. "You didn't answer my pages."

As always, I was torn between anger and flattery. "My battery died. What do you need?"

I began walking toward her office, and she fell into step next to me, her hands agitated. "Something came up and I can't make an appointment. I need you to go in my place."

I perked up—cover for Helena? Until now, she'd never asked me to do more than cover her behind. I was momentarily dazzled by her confidence in me. "Sure, Helena, I'd be happy to."

My mind spun with the possible exposure and what it could mean for my career. A Chamber of Commerce meeting? A symposium on periodicals at the Guggenheim? An advertising think tank? I was relieved I'd worn a decent suit and shoes—both a half-season old, but passable if I snagged a Hermès scarf from the prop department. "Just tell me where."

Helena smiled, all congenial and girl-friendly now. "I can always count on you, Kenzie. I have everything ready for you in my office."

My stride was instantly longer, my posture two inches taller, and I fought to control the giddy grin that threatened to burst over my face. Helena was finally making good on her promise to delegate visible assignments. If this one involved Donald Trump or the mayor, I'd simply have to endure my man allergy for the afternoon for the sake of my new assignment. A girl had to make sacrifices to get ahead.

Helena swung open the door to her office and I followed, but my elongated stride was cut short by the sight of the visitor sitting in Helena's leather guest chair. A little dog covered with hair longer than mine sat on her pretty little haunches, took one look at me, and yawned. A bad feeling settled on top of my Caesar salad.

"This is Angel," Helena sang, scooping up the pooch and bringing it close enough for me to see that the pink ribbon between its pointy little ears was silk. And Versace. "This is Kenzie," Helena cooed to the dog.

The only thing that surpassed my surprise over seeing the frou-frou dog in Helena's pristine office was the sound of my boss speaking in baby-talk. "I didn't know you had a dog."

"I bought her last night at a pet store on Fifty-Third. Isn't she adorable?"

"Adorable," I agreed.

"She's a Yorkie, a former show dog," Helena gushed. "Her ancestors belonged to royalty."

"Ah." I extended my hand for a trial stroke, and Angel emitted an un-angelic growl. I withdrew my hand.

Helena laughed. "Oh, she didn't mean that—Angel is as tame as a stuffed animal. She just needs to get to know you better. By the time you get back from Tatum's the two of you will be fast friends."

I stared at the creature that resembled a miniature version of Cousin It from the "Addams Family." "This—" I swallowed and started again. "This is the appointment you can't make?"

"Uh-huh," Helena said ruefully. "I just got a thank-you call from the mayor's office about the public service ads we ran last month on tourism—they want to get a handshake picture, and of course I couldn't say no. But Angel has an appointment at Tatum's, the *most* exclusive grooming salon in the city, and if I miss this appointment, they'll blacklist her."

I'd lived in Manhattan long enough to know that those things did happen—even the animals here had a social circle. Still, as far as executive assistant duties went, dog-sitting went a little beyond the normal tasks of picking up the dry cleaning, getting theater tickets and making dinner reservations. "Helena, I'm not a concierge. You said you were going to give me an assignment that would make a difference in my career."

Helena nodded. "You're so right, Kenzie, and I promise the next big assignment that crosses my desk will be yours. Just do me this one teensy favor."

I looked at the little mutt and groaned inwardly. "But I'm allergic to pet dander."

"I'll owe you one," Helena said in her most cajoling voice.

I sighed. "In that case, I'd like to leave the office early on Thursday."

She pursed her perfectly penciled mouth. "How early?"

I narrowed my eyes.

"I mean...it's a deal." Helena recovered with a magnanimous smile, then shoved Angel into my arms.

2

"SO WHAT did you have to do to get out of the office early?" Jacki asked me over the top of our sweet and sour margaritas. Over the past couple of years, my girlfriends and I had gone through a martini phase and a Cosmopolitan phase and now were back to good old tequila...although we *had* graduated to El Tesoro Platinum. Olé.

I didn't want to admit to the girls that I'd been reduced to a dog valet (simply thinking about the horrid afternoon at the pet salon made me flinch), so I shrugged. "Helena isn't as evil as everyone thinks. She has a soft spot." *For her pooch,* I didn't add. When I'd delivered news from the groomer that Helena should consider having Angel's wings (i.e., ovaries) clipped, my boss had been outraged. I suspected her reluctance to fix Angel had something to do with Helena's own well-publicized struggle with the onset of menopause.

And I promised myself this would be the last time I would defend my boss until the career-altering project she promised materialized. In truth, a festering resentment against Helena had been building inside me all week, and today I was feeling defiant of her and of life in general. I was thirty-one, and *Thirty-One Candles* was not the title of a movie because, as birthdays go, it was an unremarkable milestone. But I was decidedly restless and looking to be liberated from my six-month career marathon. Plus tequila always made me a tad horny. Olé.

I did a slow scan of the bar—between the regrettable one-year stint with my ex James and my new job, I'd been off the market for a while. Among the sea of faces, a boyish grin caught my eye. A sandy-haired man was chatting with the bartender and tossing back a handful of nuts. He looked out of place—woodsy almost, with his L. L. Bean T-shirt (I knew T-shirts) and sunburned cheeks. That was no tanning salon tan. He seemed to be comfortably alone—no guy (or girl) friends on the periphery, and he wasn't looking up every few seconds to see if anyone was on the make.

Like me, for instance.

"So how's your man allergy?" Cindy asked, jarring me out of my reverie.

Darn, I'd almost forgotten. "Active," I murmured, realizing that the man at the bar was just the kind of guy I normally went for. Which meant he'd probably throw my body into metabolic chaos.

"Don't tell me you're still hanging on to that pitiful excuse for not meeting men?" Jacki said.

"I'm telling you, it's for real," I insisted. "And it's for my own good."

"Well, you're going to have to risk an outbreak," Denise said, then exchanged devilish grins with Cindy and Jacki. "At least for one night."

I squinted. "What are you three up to?"

"Happy Birthday," Denise shouted, then plopped a gaily wrapped package onto the table. "It's from all of us."

"You shouldn't have," I said, but I welled with pleasure.

In my lifetime I had experienced a high rate of friend turnover because I and everyone I knew seemed to be in perpetual motion—every apartment and every job seemed eerily temporary, a pit stop to somewhere potentially more fulfilling. I had met Denise, Jacki and Cindy when we all worked for a textbook publisher over four years ago. From there our careers had taken different paths, but we had managed to stay in touch. I treasured the low-maintenance, high-gossip bond I shared with these three women.

I dutifully read the humorous card, then tore into the package thinking jewelry! Perfume! Handbag! The girls always knew just the right gift.

When the paper revealed a description of the box contents, however, I decided they must have run out of good ideas. "A Make Your Own Dildo kit?"

"Isn't it great?" Denise asked, squealing.

I stared at the box, which portrayed a woman from the waist up. Her hands were out of sight, and she looked pleased with herself. "M-make my own? I'm not much of an artist."

Jacki scoffed. "You don't *sculpt* the dildo—you make a cast."

"From what?"

"From the real thing, silly."

I gaped. "You mean...?"

They all screamed with laughter, nodding. "Since you're *allergic* to sexy men," Jacki said dryly, "we thought we'd buy you something that would kill two birds with one stone."

"First," Denise said, "you find a hot one-night stand who's willing to be commemorated in silicone."

"Then," Cindy continued, "you'll have Mr. Hot and Sexy's likeness to keep you company when you find Mr. Nice and *Un*sexy to settle down with."

Although their words made tequila-hazy sense, there

was an error in their collective logic that I felt compelled to point out. "I've never had a one-night stand."

"Well, Kenzie," Jacki said, lifting her glass, "you're not getting any younger."

I was prevented from answering by the appearance of one of the most horrific sights a woman can imagine—a small cake ablaze with what appeared to be the correct number of candles. My friends burst into an off-key rendition of "Happy Birthday," and I felt the eyes of everyone in the bar turn my way while a few tipsy bystanders chimed in. I hid the dildo kit on my lap, thinking maybe I could donate it to the Goodwill store in the red-light district.

The poor waitress nearly set her crop-top on fire as she parked the torch on our table. Since I was already lightheaded, I inhaled as deeply as I dared and managed to blow out most of the candles. Cheers sounded all over the bar.

My cheeks burned as I glanced around with a smile to simultaneously thank the strangers for their attention and apologize for the interruption. At the bar, the sandy-haired nut-eating guy had turned his engaging grin in my direction. My own smile went all watery, and when I realized that I was making way too much eye contact, I wrenched my gaze away.

But Jacki had noticed. "Quarry spotted, girls—Eagle Scout, two o'clock."

Before I could tell them not to look, they all had twisted in their seats. I sank lower in mine.

"He's perfect," Denise oozed.

"And he's looking at you, Kenzie." Cindy fluttered her hands.

I closed my eyes briefly. "Because he hasn't seen this

kind of spectacle since sixth grade." I picked up a table knife. "Why don't I cut the cake?" *Or an artery.*

Thankfully, butter-cream icing diverted the girls' attention. I cut wedges of the yellow cake and passed them all around, and there were a few extra slices for spectators who eyed the free food like starving coyotes.

I ate the cake with my hands and savored the fats and sugars that sang to my tastebuds—despite my best dietary intentions, I had a vigorous sweet tooth. I was licking the icing off my fingers when I realized that if the guy at the bar was watching, he'd think my manners were wanting...or that finger-licking was my method of bewitching a man into asking me out. My eyeballs hurt from the strain of not looking back to see if he was looking back to see if I was looking back to see if he was looking back at me, but I had discipline. I had devoured only one piece of cake, hadn't I?

I pushed the man from my thoughts and ordered us all another round of drinks. For the next hour, the girls and I dished about work and music and movies, agreeing that recycled office air was ravaging our skin, Josh Groban was the best thing that had happened to serious music in a long time, and *The Thomas Crowne Affair* was the sexiest movie of all time. Once or twice I accidentally glanced toward the bar and noticed that Eagle Scout was still there. He didn't seem to be in a hurry to leave, lingering over a steak and watching a sports channel on the TV over the bar. Something about the casual, athletic way he held his body spoke to me. I told myself a guy who looked that good had to be taken.

On the other hand, I wasn't chopped liver, and I was sleeping alone.

At that precise moment, he looked up and caught me staring. A hint of a smile curved his mouth and my heart went kaboom. I had never been so instantly and unjustifiably attracted to a man, so I blamed it on the alcohol coursing through my bloodstream and the urge to be disobedient on my birthday. I readied my most flirtatious smile, then was assailed by a violent itch on my neck that reminded me why I was still single at thirty-one—I kept picking the same kind of guy.

So I pretended to be looking at something behind the guy's broad shoulder, and rejoined my friends' conversation about the best long-lasting lipstick.

"We did a piece last month on a lady in Boston who specializes in cosmetic tattooing," I offered. "Permanent lipliner, beauty marks, even eyebrows."

Everyone paused in consideration, then winced and shook their heads. I agreed, but I wondered if I'd warm up to the idea of permanent makeup a few birthday candles down the road.

When Jacki glanced at her watch, I realized that she probably had plans with Ted later and that I should wrap things up and let her off the hook.

"Thanks for everything, girls." I glanced around at the women who had been constants in my life for over four years and felt a mushy mood coming on.

"Open the dildo kit before we leave," Denise urged.

The mushy mood vanished. "Here?"

"Just the directions," Cindy said. "I'm dying to know how this thing works."

Not wanting to seem unappreciative, I set the box on the table and, while covering as much of the wording as possible, broke the seal with my thumbnail. I raised the lid a couple of inches and studied the innocuous looking white containers and cardboard cylinder. It had all the trappings of a science project. I withdrew a pink sheet of paper with the ominous words Before Making Your Dildo, Read These Directions Carefully printed across the top.

The girls huddled close, and I was reminded of the time in fourth grade when I'd stolen the insert from my mother's box of tampons and scoured it with a friend on the school bus. In a low voice, I read the step-by-step instructions to mix the casting agent with tap water, pour the mixture into the cardboard cylinder that was closed at one end, then have the properly prepped "caster" insert his member into the cylinder, and the casting agent would harden almost instantly, creating a perfect cast when he withdrew. The final step was to fill the cast with tinted silicone, let it set for two hours, then pop out the replica dildo and "enjoy."

While the girls hugged themselves with laughter, I scanned the rest of the directions. After "enjoying," the dildo could be cleaned by placing it in the top rack of the dishwasher. Olé.

"This is going to be great," Jacki said, nodding. "You have to promise to show us the end product."

I shrugged. "Sure, but I have to warn you—I don't see any 'casting' parties in my near future."

"I don't know," Denise sang. "The guy at the bar is still looking over here."

I refused to look, but I couldn't hold back a frivolous smile. "Really?"

"But if you're going to have a one-night stand," Jacki said, "you have to know the ground rules."

"I'm not having a one-night stand," I insisted, shaking my head. Then I squinted. "There are ground rules?"

Jacki nodded. "You have to let a friend know who you'll be with."

"That's so if you're strangled, we'll be able to give the police a description," Cindy added solemnly.

"Ah."

"But don't worry—I could describe him with my eyes closed," Denise said, then closed her eyes. "Brown hair, chinos, T-shirt, cowboy hat." She opened her eyes. "How'd I do?"

"You got the T-shirt right," I offered.

Denise frowned and twisted for another steely observation. "Damn, why did I think he was wearing a cowboy hat?"

"Because he has that look," Jacki said. "Like he might lasso something." She looked at me. "Or some*one*."

I scratched. "This is not going to happen."

"Don't take him back to your place, and don't go to his," Cindy said.

"Right," Denise added. "It has to be somewhere safe and neutral—like a hotel room."

"That way he won't know where you live."

"Oh, and lie about where you work, in case he's a stalker."

"And don't give him your real last name."

"Or your real phone number."

I was dizzy from looking back and forth. "Let me get this straight—assuming the man and I have a conversation before falling into bed, I'm supposed to tell him a pack of lies?"

"Right," Denise said.

"Is he allowed to talk?"

"Sure," Jacki said. "But assume he's lying, too."

"And if you spend the night, leave before he wakes up," Denise said.

"That way you can avoid the whole awkward morning-after scene," Cindy said.

"Although leaving something for him to remember you by is a nice touch," Jacki added. "I once left an earring."

"The little rose from my bra," Cindy said dreamily.

"A garter belt," Denise admitted.

I laughed, incredulous. "If it's so much work, why bother?"

"Good sex," Jacki said.

"Great sex," Cindy said.

"Fabulous sex," Denise said. "It's very liberating to get down and dirty with someone you'll never see again."

"Right," Jacki said. "Sex with someone you love is the best, but sex with a stranger is right up there near the top of the list."

"It's kind of like being a man for one night," Cindy said. "Having great sex with no emotional attachment, no strings."

They were all nodding, and I felt ridiculously left out. A liberating experience might be just what I needed to mark an unremarkable birthday. I glanced toward the bar and the sandy-haired guy was still there, watching TV and sprawled loosely in his chair. I felt myself begin to salivate. Of course, entertaining a naughty thought was one thing—acting upon it was something else entirely. Segues had always been a problem for me. I didn't mind taking chances, but I could never seem to do it elegantly.

"*Assuming* I were to have a conversation with the guy, and *assuming* that he's available and willing to have a one-night stand—" I ignored the round of snorts "—how does one broach the subject of making a cast of a man's penis?"

Jacki shrugged. "A man is always looking for an interesting place to put it."

"Yeah," Cindy said. "Tell him he'll be immortalized in silicone, and try to *stop* him from poking into that plaster."

"Or," Denise added, pointing to the sheet of paper I held, "just show him the directions and ask him if it looks like fun."

Jacki glanced at her watch. "I have to take off. Cindy, Denise, want to share a cab?"

"Sure," they said in unison, and reached for their purses.

"I'm not staying here alone," I cried, scrambling to gather dildo kit, card, gift-wrap debris and my own bag.

Jacki made a protesting noise. "Kenzie, he isn't going to talk to you if we're in a huddle. Good*bye*." The girls waved and strode toward the door.

I glanced in the direction of the bar and the guy seemed to have noticed the commotion. He leaned forward slightly, as if he was trying to decide whether to make his move. I panicked and stood to follow my friends. But when I hit my feet, the tequila hit my adenoids and sent an air bubble to my brain. I grabbed for the table, and all my belongings fell to the floor. Something heavy hit my shoe, but I was too light-headed to do more than wince. Slowly the sparkly feeling subsided and I blinked the Eagle Scout into view. If anything, he was even nicer looking up close.

"Are you all right?" he asked in a warm, husky voice.

Thick hair the color of antique brass, wide cheekbones, sun-bleached eyebrows...and shiny brown bedroom eyes. The moisture evaporated from my mouth, and pure desire bolted through me. "I...yes."

He flashed that killer smile, and my knees turned to elastic. At the same time, we bent to gather my wayward items. Thank heavens the dildo kit box had landed face-down, but its contents—canisters of the casting agent and the silicone—had rolled away. He retrieved them with long, tanned arms, and handed them to me. When our fingers touched, my heart raced, and my ears rang like wedding—er, *church* bells. Spending time with this man would be hazardous to my plan of finding a nice unsexy guy to settle down with. I was already half in love with him and I didn't even know his name.

While covering the words on the box, I stuffed the canisters inside and stood, trying to act as nonchalantly as possible. "Thank you, um—"

"Sam," he said.

Nice name. "Thank you. Sam." His friendly eyes held an invitation that promised to have me on an antihistamine drip.

"And you are?"

"Just leaving," I said with a tight smile. It was for my own good.

"Oh." He seemed disappointed, but accepting. "Well...happy birthday."

"Thank you."

"Nice almost meeting you."

I experienced a pang of regret because the man emanated sexual vibes that my body honed in on. "Nice almost meeting you, too."

I turned to go, telling myself I might meet my nice unsexy settling-down guy while I waited for a cab.

"Hey," he called. "You forgot something."

I turned back and, to my horror, saw him bending to retrieve the pink sheet of paper with the Make Your Own Dildo directions written on it. The subhead—The Only Kit That Lets You Cast It from the Real Thing—seemed to jump off the page. I lunged for the paper, but Sam was too quick for my tequila-diluted mobility. When he lifted his gaze from the sheet, a mischievous smile curved his mouth and his eyes danced. "Looks like fun."

Desire gripped me and I mentally reviewed the ground rules for a one-night stand. Olé.

3

WHEN I JERKED AWAKE, sunlight was streaming through the crack in the curtains of the hotel room and Sam's warm breath bathed my shoulder blade. I enjoyed two seconds of blissful afterglow until panic seized me like a giant hand, squeezing the air out of my lungs. What time was it? I bolted upright and a tiny tequila bomb exploded inside my head. I carefully raked the hair out of my eyes, searching for a clock. Next to me, Sam moaned and reached out an arm—presumably for me. I put a pillow under his hand, and he seemed content to pull it close and fall back into a dead sleep.

So much for being irreplaceable.

Holding my head, I left the bed, trying not to disturb him, and trying not to shriek in my mounting fear that I was probably late for work. The air-conditioner vent was blowing like an arctic breeze—I was naked and freezing and my thigh muscles screamed from overuse as I limped around the room looking for my watch, my underwear and my mind. What had I been thinking to spend the night with a stranger in his hotel room? I felt like a...dirty girl.

I found my watch on a table under a pile of clothes, and nearly swallowed my tongue—I had ten minutes to dress and get to work on time. Helena would have my head.

I scooped up the pile of clothes and my bag that doubled as briefcase and purse, then sprinted into the bathroom, closing the door behind me before flipping on the light. I stared blinking into the mirror, horrified at my reflection—my blond hair stood on end and my eyes were mascara-rimmed. Worse, with my kiss-swollen mouth and heavy-lidded eyes, I looked as if I'd just had the best night of sex in my life.

Which was true.

Except my swollen lips and heavy eyes were actually manifestations of the allergic reaction that had claimed my body—they perfectly complemented the hives raised on my neck and chest. I was allergic to big Sam, big time.

While I ran enough water in the sink for a quick wash up, I tried not to dwell on the image of Sam's bronze body wrapped around mine, and the amazing things he'd done to me. Granted, not dwelling was easier said than done considering that sitting on the sink vanity was the cardboard cylinder that held the cast we'd made of Sam's...*you know.* Hardened flesh-colored silicone seeped from the end of the cast impression, and I was dying to see how the dildo had turned out, but getting ready for work took priority.

I downed aspirin from my handbag and willed it to kick in quickly. With soap and a washcloth, I gave my body a quick once-over, then rummaged in Sam's leather toiletry bag for deodorant. The sporty scent might raise a few eyebrows, but it was better than the alternative. I pulled makeup basics from my purse, and applied it all in record time, then squirted perfume on my wrists. The hives were itching like crazy, but I knew scratching would only make them worse.

I pulled my haphazard hair back into a twist and secured it with the only clasp I could find in my purse—a banker's clip. It would have to do until I could grab something from the prop room at work. Then I sorted through the clothes with dread in my stomach. If I showed up wearing the same clothes I'd worn yesterday, I might as well wear a sign that read I Got Laid Last Night. I opted not to wear the same pair of panties, reckoning that my pantyhose would be enough of a barrier between me and my slacks for decency's sake. But my blouse was stained with makeup from yanking it over my head last night, and I hadn't worn a jacket.

I eyed the closet next to the shower and peeked inside to find a beautiful tan-colored suit, white dress shirt, and geometric tie hanging under plastic. I was surprised because Sam didn't seem like the suit type—he'd told me he was a doctor visiting from out of town, but hadn't Jacki said to assume he was lying? I had certainly lied, as instructed, including telling him my last name was Moore.

With murmured apologies, I slid the dress shirt from the plastic, shrugged into it, rolled up the sleeves, secured it wrap-style, and tucked it inside my navy slacks. I used the geometric tie as a belt, then glanced into the mirror. Not bad for a ten-minute session—as long as no one looked too closely.

I stuffed my makeup bag, blouse and panties into my bag and prepared to dash out the door when I remembered the "cast." Since I'd never see Sam again, I was definitely taking that souvenir with me. But when I hefted the cardboard cylinder that held the hardened cast, I realized it was too heavy to lug around and would take up too much room in my bag. So I slipped my fingers under the mound of silicone at the base of the cast, and after a couple of tugs, pulled out the dildo with a *pop*.

I gasped. Granted, the kit had said the dildo would be lifelike, but...*damn*. It was indeed an exact replica of Sam's finest physical asset. A splendid springy, firm, flesh-colored replica that brought tingly memories flooding back to various parts of my body. I had lucked out when

I'd chosen Sam as the "caster." This baby was going on display in my china cabinet.

After a couple of appreciative strokes, I shoved the homemade dildo into my bag, flipped off the light, and opened the door as quietly as I could. In the semi-darkness, Sam was still snuggled up to the pillow. I conceded a stab of desire just looking at his long lean body in the twisted sheets. The chemistry between us had been magical, but I knew that the intensity of our lovemaking had more to do with the fact that we'd never see each other again than with any kind of kismet. Besides, the unbearable itching on my chest was proof enough that my body would be in a constant state of chaos if I spent any time at all with the man.

Still...the romantic in me wanted to believe that our one-night stand was better than any one-night stand in history. I had the overwhelming urge to push the hair off his forehead and kiss him goodbye, but gave myself a mental shake. I did, however, recall what Jacki said about leaving a memento. I needed my earrings to look halfway put together, my bra didn't have an embroidered flower, and I didn't own a garter belt.

But in my bag I had a pair of pink imported French panties that had held Sam's attention for quite a while before he'd removed them with his teeth. The expensive undies seemed like a fair trade for the dress shirt.

I dropped the panties on the side of the bed I'd slept on, glanced around to make sure I had my belongings, and walked to the door as soundlessly as I could. I looked back at Sam's sleeping form and experienced a twinge of regret that I hadn't shared enough information about myself or found out enough about him for us ever to connect again. And even though it was probably against the rules, I blew him a wistful kiss.

I wasn't very good at this one-night-stand business.

And I was late for work. I took the elevator to the lobby and dashed through it with my head down, sure that everyone knew what I'd done. I walked faster and faster, which only brought into play more and more muscles that I'd overworked last night and aggravated my booming headache. And apparently Sam liked heavy starch—the collar of his shirt chafed my neck, and the fabric was wreaking havoc on my hives. Some part of me, though, felt as if I deserved to be miserable after what I'd done. Mind you, I'm not a virginal prude, but deep down I still wanted to believe that sex was a special, intimate experience with emotional fallout. To realize that I had so enjoyed the purely physical encounter left me questioning what I knew to be true about myself.

I hailed a cab and slid into the lobby of the Woolworth Building a mere fifteen minutes late, but I felt as though the day had started without me. My nerves clanged and I wondered what Helena had manufactured for me to do today to make up for the fact that I'd left early yesterday. Fridays were notoriously busy so that those who would be working over the weekend could get the assignments that they had to complete for Monday morning. I wasn't surprised when I walked into my closet-office to the tune of my phone ringing.

I set my bag on my desk and yanked up the receiver. "Kenzie Mansfield."

"*Well?*" Jacki asked.

One side of my mouth slid back. "Well, what?"

"Well, how was the Eagle Scout?"

"I knew I shouldn't have left you that message."

"It was the safe thing to do. Did you spend the night?"

I sighed. "Yes."

"And how was it?"

"Great," I admitted.

"You don't sound too excited. Did he refuse to be *cast?*"

I glanced toward my bag where the lifelike dildo resided. "Uh, no, he was...*up* for the job."

"And?"

"And it worked perfectly."

"I'm going to order a kit for me and Ted as soon as I hang up." She paused. "Why are you so glum—was he...*petite?*"

I laughed and dropped into my chair. "No, he was not *petite.* I'm just feeling out of sorts. My head is hammering, I woke up too late to go back to my apartment, I had to wear his shirt to the office—"

"You weren't supposed to talk to him this morning!"

"I didn't."

"You *stole* the guy's shirt?"

I mourned my pink Lejaby panties. "More like traded for it. Anyway...I don't know, Jacki, it was really weird to sleep with this guy and just get up and leave, knowing I'll never see him again."

"Maybe you will run into him again."

"He said he's from out of town."

"He probably lied. For all you know, he could work in the mailroom of your building."

"Running into him would be even worse. How awkward would that be?"

"Pretty awkward if he has you arrested for stealing his shirt. Wait a minute—do you have *feelings* for this guy?"

I blinked. "*No*—unless itchy feelings count. I have hives."

"That sounds attractive."

"Let's just say I don't think I'll be having any more one-night stands." I fiddled with one of the buttons on Sam's shirt. "I guess I want what you have with Ted."

"And you'll find it," Jacki said. "Last night was just an exercise to jumpstart your social life."

"I hope you're right," I mumbled.

"And look on the bright side—you have the guy's silicone portrait to remember him by."

I was minutely cheered. "I have to admit it's one beautiful dildo."

A shadow darkened my door and I looked up to see Helena standing there, holding a stack of file folders. Wondering how much she'd heard, I fixed my face into a serious expression and adopted a professional tone to pretend I was on a business call. "I'll have to look into that and get back to you later." I hung up, made a bogus note on scratch paper, then turned a sunny smile toward my boss. "Good morning."

"You're late."

"I...was caught in traffic. Sorry."

Helena squinted. "Is that a banker's clip in your hair?"

I stood and pointed to the files. "Something I can take off your hands?"

Helena gave me a suspicious look, then nodded and handed me the files. "Could you please take a look at these circulation reports and have a summary for me by this afternoon?"

I blinked because I didn't realize the word *please* was in Helena's vocabulary. "Sure, I'll have a report for you ASAP."

Helena started to go, then turned back. "Kenzie, did you enjoy your time off yesterday?"

I smiled at her cordial tone. "Yes, I did."

"Is there anything you'd like to...share?"

My throat constricted. Was it that obvious that I'd recently crawled out of a strange bed and sponged the sex off my body before donning stolen clothes and sliding into the office late? "I...no."

She gave me another wary once-over, then turned and strode away. I was shaking when I rummaged in my desk drawer for an antihistamine tablet. Helena could be a demanding boss, but I admired her and wanted her respect. I didn't have to consult a shrink to know that I had some kind of maternal projection complex where the woman was concerned. On the other hand, having a moral compass in one's life wasn't such a terrible thing.

I was a bad, bad girl.

But I'd had a good, good time.

In fact, I could still feel Sam's hands on my body, the rough texture of the calluses on his broad fingers—one of the reasons I'd doubted his story about being a doctor, although I couldn't argue on the subject of his dexterity. I closed my eyes and allowed myself to relive his kisses and his attention to detail—James had never made love to me like that.

Of course, James and I had never had a one-night stand. Maybe men simply performed better during one-night stands without the pressure of a repeat performance hanging over their heads. In fact, there was probably a woman out there who'd had a one-night stand with James and sat in her office with her eyes closed, fantasizing about his freakishly small hands.

Or maybe not.

The break room was on the other end of the department, but I dragged myself over there to fill a huge insulated mug with strong, hot coffee. The milk container in the mini-fridge was empty, so I braved the brew straight. My spirits lifted, though, when I spotted a lone powdered sugar doughnut on a plate. My stomach howled and I wondered if Sam had ordered room service.

"What are you smiling about?"

I turned to see April Bromley coming into the room, smothering a yawn. My hackles raised. April was the executive assistant to the creative director, Ron Castle, and she was always trying to usurp what scrap of authority I had. She was a dark, exotic goddess and was not above using her considerable curves to further her ambitions. We didn't like each other, and we didn't hide it.

"I'm smiling because I love my job," I said sweetly.

"So do I," she returned just as sweetly. "But I could never do your job, Kenzie—I don't like dogs."

A flush climbed my face as a triumphant smile crawled over hers. Apparently word of my stint as a dog-sitter had reached the water cooler.

April grabbed the doughnut I'd had my eye on, took a bite, and shrugged prettily. "I need energy for the meeting that Ron asked me to sit in on this morning. If we need any copies made during the meeting, I'm sure Helena will buzz you."

I looked for something to buzz *her* with, but she'd already flounced out. Ooh! That woman knew how to push my buttons, knew that Helena never invited me to sit in on the creative meetings. And since I had to write that summary report, this morning didn't seem like a good time to hint for an invitation.

That's why I was shocked when about thirty minutes later, while I was elbow-deep in circulation reports, Helena called and asked me to sit in on the creative meeting.

"You're one of my most valued employees, Kenzie. It's time that you became familiar with what the other departments are doing."

So Helena was feeling guilty about the dog-sitting gig—good. I could only imagine the look on April's face when I walked into the meeting, but I tried to keep the elation out of my voice and still sound conscientious. "What's on the agenda?"

"Ron is finalizing the cover for an upcoming issue."

A sore spot with Helena—after several incarnations, she still wasn't happy with the cover look for *Personality.* From my perspective, finalizing a cover was one of the more interesting steps in producing a weekly news magazine. Still, I manufactured a thoughtful noise. "That sounds great, but I'd like to finish the summary report first."

"Oh."

Helena was caught off guard—she thought I'd be frothing at the mouth to join the meeting. I was, but she didn't have to know that.

"The meeting will last until noon. Join us in the west boardroom when you can."

"I will." I hung up the phone feeling pretty pleased with myself and at least a birthday wiser. Helena was definitely treating me differently today. Maybe last night had been a turning point for me—a bon voyage of sorts to my immature fantasy of what the world was like. Goodbye multiple orgasms, hello functional sex. So long French panties, hello sensible underwear. It was time to advance my career, and find a marriageable man.

I suddenly felt very grown-up.

I pulled out my Palm Pilot and called up my to-do list for the following Monday. Using the stylus, I wrote "Start looking for a nice guy" on the screen, then stabbed the tiny enter button as ardently as possible, breaking a nail. Still, I was resolute.

I finished the reports five minutes before the meeting started, but I decided to wait another fifteen minutes before making my entrance. I lifted the lapel of Sam's shirt and was happy to see that the hives had all but disappeared. After refilling my drum of black coffee, I gathered a fresh pad of paper and a pen, and walked to the meeting room.

A hum of voices floated through the closed door. I checked my clothing and smoothed a hand over my hair. My heartbeat was clicking away, and I prayed I could make at least one intelligent remark over the course of the meeting. I twisted the doorknob and entered as quietly as possible (I was doing a lot of sneaking in and out of rooms today), taking mental stock of the attendees—Helena, Ron Castle, April and a dozen others from production, photography, editorial and marketing. I claimed the closest empty chair, tucking myself in and turning toward the speaker, Ron.

He paused and gave me an inquisitive look akin to "What are *you* doing here?" A flush scorched my cheeks as all eyes landed on me. April smirked.

"Everyone knows my assistant, Kenzie Mansfield," Helena spoke up. "I asked Kenzie to sit in because I'd like to begin exposing her to more activities in various departments."

I circulated a respectful smile, stopping short of April, then Ron picked up where he'd left off.

"As I was saying, I think the hometown hero issue is going to be a big success in terms of attracting new readers—high-earning blue-collar workers who might not normally pick up a copy of *Personality* will be attracted by the all-American appeal of this issue."

"The advertising department is on board," offered Nita, the marketing manager. "Banks, insurance companies and car manufacturers are lining up for this issue."

"The difficult part," Ron continued, "was finding just the right person for the cover." Then he smiled. "But I think we've found a winner—a volunteer firefighter from Jar Hollow, New York."

"Where's that?" Helena asked.

"It's a speck of a town between Albany and Syracuse, genuine mom-and-pop stuff. This guy rushed into a nursing home fire and saved a dozen patients."

Nathan from production snapped his fingers. "I heard about him on TV—the governor's giving him some kind of medal."

"The governor offered," Ron corrected, "but the guy wouldn't accept it. Said he was just doing what any American would do."

"He sounds perfect," Helena said. "Tell me he's marginally photogenic."

Ron glanced at his watch. "I'll let you judge for yourself if he ever gets here. April, could you run down and check with the receptionist to see if Mr. Long has arrived? And while you're at it, could you make an extra copy of the agenda for Kenzie?"

I wanted to cackle, but I schooled my face into a sedate expression. April's eyes shot daggers in my direction, but she skedaddled like a good little go-fer.

"We'll have some convincing to do," Ron said. "This Long guy isn't keen on all the attention he's been getting."

"Nonsense," Helena snapped. "Everyone likes attention. He'll do it."

Since everyone knew Helena got whatever she wanted, the matter seemed closed. Ron and the marketing director then passed around alternative layouts for the upcoming issue.

"I think the configuration with fewer words is cleaner," Ron said.

"It really makes the cover image pop," Nita added.

Helena studied the new look, then slid the mock-up in my direction. "Kenzie, what do you think?"

The silence was profound, although no one in the room

was more surprised by her question than I. Still, the fact that it was the first time I'd been asked in a public forum for my opinion did not mean that I hadn't been saving up. I took a deep breath.

"The more words, the better—it makes the buyer feel as if there's a lot of content. Mix up the fonts and colors to entertain the customer's eye, but reduce the font size of the price so it seems insignificant. Using multiple colors for the magazine title would be a nice change of pace—maybe red, white and blue for this issue. Adopting an exclamation mark at the end of the magazine title could be an effective visual cue. And an occasional short-fold cover would be an attention-getter, not to mention adding premium space for advertisers."

I exhaled into the hush of the room, but as I glanced from one bemused face to another, I fervently wished for a rewind button. "Or not," I murmured.

The door opened, and as much as I disliked April, I was glad for her timely return.

"I found our cover model," she gushed. "Everyone, this is Mr. Samuel Long."

A well-suited man with hair the color of antique brass stepped in the room and flashed an engaging grin. My vital signs stalled. It couldn't be.

Oh. But. It. Was.

4

"WELCOME, Mr. Long," Helena said, standing and extending her hand. "I'm Helena Birch, editor-in-chief here at *Personality*."

"Actually, it's *Dr.* Long," Sam said with no trace of conceit. Indeed, he seemed a bit flustered by all the attention. "I apologize for the delay—I'm afraid I had a bit of a wardrobe predicament this morning."

It was then that his gaze landed on me. I knew my eyes were as big as Ping-Pong balls, so I was thankful that he had the presence of mind not to say, "Hey, look, it's my one-night stand." A slight lift of his eyebrow was the only indication that he recognized me. Was that amusement in his eyes? Then his gaze lowered to my shirt—er, make that *his* shirt.

"A wardrobe predicament?" April tossed her hair. "Nonsense—you look terrific."

I frowned. *Down, girl.* Indeed, Sam had compensated rather nicely for his missing dress shirt. Underneath his creamy tan-colored suit, he wore a brown L. L. Bean T-shirt (I knew T-shirts). He pulled his gaze away from *our* shirt and gave April a little smile. "Thank you. If I've learned nothing else from being a small-town veterinarian, I've learned how to be resourceful."

"Dr. Long," Helena said, "allow me to introduce some of my staff." She made the rounds, with those closest to Sam rising to shake his hand. Including me.

"This is my assistant, Kenzie Mansfield."

"Ms. *Mansfield,*" he said, clasping my hand in his.

The brush of his wonderfully callused fingers against mine sent a pang of nostalgia to my thighs. "Welcome, Dr. Long."

His eyes danced and a corner of his mouth jerked. Beneath his shirt, my hives were being resurrected. Afraid that I might start panting aloud, I withdrew my hand.

"I'm happy to be here," Sam said, then turned back to April. "But there must be some kind of mistake, because when we walked in I thought I heard you say I was a *cover model?*"

Helena stepped up and offered a dazzling smile. "We've been discussing our upcoming small-town-hero issue, and you would be perfect for the cover, Dr. Long."

A frown marred his handsome face. "I don't know—"

"Think of the exposure it will bring to you and your town."

He scratched his temple and emitted a little laugh. "I believe I might have had enough *exposure* to last a while."

His glance flitted in my direction, and I suspected he regretted volunteering to have his wing-ding cast for posterity. I glanced around the room for an escape route. The window looked inviting.

"You don't have to make a decision now," Helena cajoled. "Let us take a few photos and finish your interview, and we'll discuss it again later after you've had time to consider the advantages."

"Dr. Long," Ron said, "April will assist you this morning during your photo shoot and interview."

April perked up like a cheerleader, and thrust her big, round pom-poms in Sam's direction.

"Ron," Helena said. "I'd like for Kenzie to join April and Dr. Long. It'll be good experience."

Alarm took hold of me. I wasn't sure what terrified me

the most—spending the morning with April or with Sam. A choking noise erupted from my throat, but I managed to turn it into a hacking cough. "I have...something... planned this morning that I...can't get out of."

Helena pursed her mouth. "Kenzie, why don't you and I get some more coffee?"

I picked up my gigantic coffee mug that was still full and followed her out of the boardroom, but we stopped a little short of the break room, as I suspected we would.

Helena crossed her arms, and pinned me to the wall with her stare. "Kenzie, earlier this week you were begging for assignments that would further your career, and when I give you one, you manufacture an excuse to get out of it. Is something wrong?"

What could I say? "No."

"Then what do you have planned that's more important than broadening your experience at the magazine?"

She was right. "Nothing."

Helena nodded. "Good. Then I expect that you and Dr. Long and April will have an enlightening time."

"Of course," I murmured. "Thank you."

Uncrossing her arms, Helena flicked nothing off her sleeve. "By the way, you had some clever ideas in there regarding the magazine's cover. Put it all in a memo and have it on my desk Monday."

Taking advantage of my speechlessness, she turned to go back to the boardroom.

"Oh, and Kenzie?"

I looked up. "Yes."

"Try to keep April from devouring Dr. Long. We're a newsmagazine—the last thing we need is a scandal that we're offering *compensation* to our sources."

I broke out into a warm sweat that tested my sport-scent deodorant. "Will do."

TWENTY MINUTES LATER, April and Sam and I were on our way to photography, me lagging behind. I was a nervous freaking wreck, and April's chattering made things worse. She hung all over Sam, and Sam looked like an animal with its leg caught in a trap. I could feel his gaze on me, and I could feel his effect on my body.

"So," April oozed, "you're a fireman."

"No, I'm a veterinarian," Sam said easily. "I'm a volunteer fireman in my spare time."

April flapped her long, curly eyelashes. "So are there a lot of fires to put out in Jar Hollow?"

Sam grinned, warming up to the attention. "Um, thankfully, no."

"But you saved all those people—that's so cool."

Two steps behind them, I rolled my eyes.

"I was in the right place at the right time," he said, then slowed and looked back, apparently determined that I should catch up.

I picked up my leaden feet and fell in step next to them. I walked on one side of Sam, April on the other, making a big, juicy Sam sandwich. Sipping lukewarm coffee from my mug, I tried to force from my mind the image of his naked body sliding against mine. I decided it might be a good idea to join the conversation. "I assume you didn't expect to become such a media sensation, Dr. Long?"

He shot a surprised glance my way. "She speaks."

I flushed because he knew good and well that not only did I speak, but on occasion, I screamed.

Sam smiled and shook his head. "You're right. Beyond the local media, I didn't think about it. Then a freelance writer called and said he'd like to do an interview for a possible segment in your magazine. We talked on the phone for a while, but when I didn't hear anything else, I assumed the story wasn't picked up." He shrugged. "Then two days ago I received a call and a plane ticket, asking me to come to the city to finalize details. So, here I am." He looked at me with brown eyes that were so deep, I felt a bout of vertigo coming on.

"Is this your first trip to Manhattan?" April asked.

"Yes," Sam and I answered in unison.

Sam bit back a smile, and April frowned in confusion. I scrambled to cover my gaffe. "I think I read that somewhere."

"And how do you like the city, Sam—may I call you Sam?" April asked adorably.

"Sure," he said. "The city is...interesting. More so even than I expected."

"Will you be staying a few days?" April's tone indicated she hoped so.

He shook his handsome head. "I arrived yesterday and I'm leaving this afternoon."

April pouted. "I hope you did something fun last night."

I lifted my coffee mug for a deep drink.

"Well," he said, his voice caramel-coated, "the evening started out slow, but it ended with a bang."

I inhaled sharply, and got coffee instead of air, which my body expelled with a painful snough (sneeze-cough). Worse, I spilled coffee down the front of my—er, his—snowy-white shirt. The brown stain spread like a virus until it was the shape of the state of Texas and nearly as big.

"Sam, I'm so sorry," I said, wiping futilely at the stain with my hand. "I'll have it cleaned." Then I froze and lifted my gaze. "May I, um, call you Sam...Sam?"

He pushed his cheek out with his tongue. "Sure."

April was looking at me as if I'd gone mad. "Kenzie, I'm sure Sam couldn't care less about your shirt."

"I m-meant that I'm sorry to have caused such a mess."

"That's okay," Sam said, then made a rueful noise. "Too bad about the shirt, though. It looks custom-made."

I balked. "It is? I mean—it *is.* But I'll contact the tailor and order another one." As soon as I could afford it.

Sam smothered a smile and nodded toward the restrooms we were approaching. "Do you need a moment, Ms. Mansfield?"

I needed a drink, but a moment would have to do. "Thank you." I race-walked into the ladies' room and leaned into the vanity, trying to pull myself together. I could get through this. The man could have blown my cover a half-dozen times by now, and he hadn't—there was nothing to fear.

So why was my heart racing like a bike messenger's?

Because I had assumed I'd never see him again, much less at work.

Work—that eighty-hours-a-week pastime that paid for groceries, rent, medical insurance and the occasional Dior accessory. I really needed not to be fired for fraternizing with an upcoming feature.

I puffed out my cheeks and studied my reflection—big-eyed and blotchy, wearing an exceptionally stained, stolen shirt, my hair skimmed back with a banker's clip. I had looked better. I poured my coffee down the sink drain—no more caffeine for me—then I practiced a few deep-breathing techniques. I needed to calm down, or Sam might think that last night had meant something to me. So our one-night stand had turned into a one-night-and-next-day stand—so what? A few more hours, then I would never see him again.

I splashed cold water on my wrists, tried to blot out the stain, then walked out feeling refreshed if not relaxed.

April stood in the hall alone. I had a panicky thought that Sam had spilled the beans and vamoosed.

"Dr. Long had to make a phone call," April said.

Oh, God—he was calling the police.

"Some kind of animal emergency," she added in a bored voice, then inspected her manicure. "Listen, Kenzie, if you want to bow out, I'll make your excuses when Sam comes back."

I had to hand it to her—she had the innocent act down pat. "Nice try, April, but you heard what Helena said. She wants me to learn more about the business." And to chaperone.

April's innocent act vanished and she gave me a pitying look. "I guess this *is* a step up from dog-sitting."

I gritted my teeth.

"But keep your hands off *this* puppy," she warned. "He's mine."

I was, oh, so tempted to tell her that not only had I had already put my hands on this puppy, but I had a duplicate of his bone in my bag upstairs. Still, I couldn't resist asking, "What makes you think Dr. Long is even available?"

"*Every* man is available."

"He's leaving after lunch."

"Plans change," she said, her voice shrill. "Besides, I think he likes me."

Jealousy tweaked me. I couldn't stand April, but from a male point of view, what was not to like? She was gorgeous and voluptuous—and did I mention gorgeous? If April had been at Fitzgerald's last night, Sam would have stepped over me to get to her.

"It's never good to mix business with pleasure," I said, knowing how lame my words sounded. And hypocritical.

April gave me a look of disgust. "When was the last time you got laid, Kenzie?"

A cough sounded behind us. We turned to see that Sam had returned. I closed my eyes briefly—how much had he overheard?

"Sorry about the interruption," he said. "Minor emergency back home."

"Is everything okay?" I asked.

"Fine, thanks. Jeremy Daly's pig swallowed a spoon, but it's no big deal—I can take care of it tomorrow."

Spoon-swallowing sounded serious to me, but he looked cheerful enough. "Alrighty then—shall we proceed to the studio?" I sneezed ferociously—three times.

Sam removed a handkerchief from an inside jacket pocket and handed it to me. "Are you getting a cold?"

"Allergies," I mumbled.

5

"I THINK I'm in love," April breathed.

Looking around the studio, I decided that every single person present was mesmerized by Dr. Sam Long, hometown hero. The photo director had decided it would be a good idea for editorial to finish the interview during the shoot, so the pictures would look more natural. I was happy for the chance to see a staff writer in action, but I had to admit that I was also perversely interested in the information being drawn out of said subject.

"I grew up in upstate New York. I went to Cornell to study veterinary science, and after I graduated, I wound up in Albany specializing in equine research." His engaging smile then faltered a bit. "I loved my work, but the pace was hectic. A couple of years went by and I began to have chest pains. I was diagnosed with a faulty heart valve."

I felt an inexplicable stab of alarm.

"Did you have surgery?" the writer asked.

"No. The problem is inoperable, but my doctor said I'd be fine as long as my lifestyle improved." He lifted his arms in an appealing shrug and the photographer clicked away. "So I looked for a small town where I could start a vet practice, and Jar Hollow was the place I found."

"Sounds like Mayberry."

He nodded. "It's a quiet lifestyle, but I enjoy it." Then he laughed. "Actually, I started feeling as if I had *too* much time on my hands, which is why I became a volunteer firefighter."

"That doesn't present a problem with your heart condition?"

"Not for as infrequently as I'm called," he said. "My doctor said the real danger is constant, prolonged stress." He grinned. "That's why I'm still single."

A round of laughter sounded, and the photographer clicked more shots. I swore his gaze flickered in my direction.

"He looked at me," April said, sitting up straighter. "I told you he was interested."

I glanced sideways at her. "It would never work out between you two."

"Why not?"

"Because you don't like dogs, remember?" I made a mock regretful noise.

She smirked. "Probably just as well—with a heart condition, he wouldn't last one night in bed with me."

I frowned. How could she do that—insult me without even knowing she was insulting me? I decided I would have to tell Jacki to add a new ground rule: determine if your one-night stand has a heart condition before signing on.

"Tell me about the nursing home fire," the writer said to Sam.

"I was in town picking up supplies. I drove by the nursing home, saw the smoke, and called 911. But the building is an old wooden structure, so I knew I couldn't stand by and wait for the fire truck to arrive."

"What did you do?"

"I had my gear in the back of my pickup—"

"He drives a pickup," April whispered. "Isn't that exotic?"

"Shh," I hissed.

"—so I began the evacuation."

"You make it sound routine," the writer said.

"It was," Sam said easily, "until some of the patients became confused. I went in and led them to safety."

"Again, you're very blasé about it."

Sam shrugged. "I'm not trying to make light of a serious situation, but I only did what anyone would have done under the circumstances. I'm just very glad that everyone is okay."

"Correction," April said with a moan. "I *know* I'm in love."

I might have been ready to swoon myself, if I hadn't been wound up as tight as a twisted rubber band. I looked at my watch, willing the hands to speed along. Every minute I spent in this man's company, I grew more and more antsy. I couldn't look at him, and I couldn't look away. I vacillated between wishing last night had never happened, and wishing it could happen again—which was absurd. Oh, sure, the more the man talked, the more I admired him. But the more he revealed about his life, the more he painted a picture of a world vastly different than mine. Plus my body's defense mechanisms had kicked in—my nose ran and my eyes watered painfully. Still, snatches of scenes from the night before replayed in my mind, as if I were pushing a feel-good button over and over.

By the time the session ended, I was a mess. I was tempted to bail on joining them for lunch, but April was so worked up after Sam put on a fire helmet and yellow jacket from the props department, I was afraid she might set herself on fire just to get him to douse her with something. Besides, Sam would be leaving after lunch, so our time together was almost up. And I had to admit that a small part of me was hoping I would get to talk to him in private, to say...well, something brilliant, I hoped.

"I need to drop by my office to get my bag," I said.

"I'll go with you," Sam said.

April looked at us suspiciously.

My mind raced. "Yes...and I'll take you to speak with Helena about the cover."

We maintained a tense silence as we stepped off the elevator and April reluctantly veered toward her office with the promise to meet us in twenty minutes. I counted, and he waited a full six seconds before breaking the silence with a hammer.

"Was this a setup?"

I stared. Of all the things I'd imagined he'd say when we were alone, that wasn't on the list. "Excuse me?"

"Did you know who I was when you saw me last night?"

"What? No!" My nervousness fled and irritation landed on my head. "Trust me, no one was more surprised than I was when you walked into that meeting this morning."

His expression was wry. "'Trust me,' says the woman who pilfered my dress shirt."

I crossed my arms. "I left you...something."

"I know. And while they were lovely and special, I couldn't very well wear them to the meeting."

A flush started at my knees and worked its way up. The elevator doors opened and three people alighted, talking amongst themselves. I lowered my voice. "Let's continue this discussion in my office, shall we?"

I led him to my office and waves of humiliation rolled over me as I gestured for him to step inside the cramped closet-sized space. There was barely room for the both of us and my desk. I don't know that I would have consciously remembered the musky clean scent of him, but when it reached my nose, my body responded like one of Pavlov's dogs. His smile wavered and I had the feeling that he, too, was remembering how intensely our bodies had connected last night. I tried to remember what we had been talking about in the hall, but I seemed to have left my brain out there. Absently, I reached up to play with my shirt collar, and remembered.

"I'm sorry about taking your shirt. I overslept and my blouse was stained, and I..."

His eyes danced. "Didn't want everyone to know you hadn't been home?"

I shrugged, cheeks flaming. "I guess I'm not very good at...this."

"Don't worry about the shirt," he said, giving it a once-over. "Even stained, it never looked so good."

My mouth went dry.

"I could get used to having you around."

I blinked. "Huh?"

He gestured to my pristine desk and hanging file system. "My home office is a wreck. I need your organization skills."

"Oh." I cleared my throat. "Listen, Dr.—Sam. You have to believe me that I didn't know who you were when I...met you last night."

He pulled on his chin. "Okay. What happened to the science project?"

I involuntarily glanced toward my purse, then back.

He followed my glance. "So you took that, too."

I squirmed. "It was my birthday present, after all."

"I suppose you're right." He picked up my favorite pen lying on my desk and studied it with little-boy fascination. "And did it turn out...accurately?"

I bit the inside of my cheek to suppress my smile. Samuel Long, Cornell grad, veterinarian and bona fide hero, was still a man. "I'd say that it is a reasonable facsimile."

He looked at me and his grin was so sexy, I had that teenager-wanna-squeal feeling.

"I only ask," he said, "because what if I agree to be on the cover of your magazine and then you go public with my *facsimile?* I wouldn't want to be embarrassed."

We laughed, and I decided that he couldn't be for real. No man was this...incredible...and single...and in proximity to *me.* As quickly as we'd burst into laughter, we got quiet again. He moved closer and I...I...sneezed three times in succession, effectively ending whatever the moment might have become.

"That's some allergy," he said as I blew my nose on his handkerchief.

"I should take my antihistamine before we go to lunch," I said, rummaging in my desk drawer.

"Have you ever considered a natural remedy?"

"Don't worry," I said. "I'll feel better in a few hours." I suspected that my recovery would coincide with Sam's departure.

We stopped by Helena's office, and she was her gracious self, but Sam still wouldn't commit to having his picture on the cover.

"I'll need your answer by tomorrow," Helena said. "And I trust it will be 'yes.'"

"I'll let you know," he said.

"Helena just purchased a Yorkie," I said.

He smiled. "Did you?"

The look that came over Helena's face was not unlike a proud parent. "Yes, she's adorable."

"How old?"

"Almost ten months."

"Ah. I hope you've had her spayed," he said.

A furrow appeared in Helena's brow. "Not yet."

"It's the right thing to do unless you're going to breed her."

Helena's shoulders went back. "I'll...think about it."

"Helena, would you like to join us for lunch?" I asked, mostly to change the subject.

She hesitated, then shook her head. "No, thank you. I'm expecting a phone call from the west coast. You'll be in good hands with Kenzie, Dr. Long."

"I don't doubt that," Sam said mildly.

"Kenzie," Helena said, eyeing my stained shirt with a frown, "you may wear my jacket to lunch." She looked back to her work, and I obediently removed her silver-gray Fendi jacket from her valet stand in the corner and escaped.

As we walked back toward the elevator, I slid my arms reverently into the jacket, with Sam's help. "My boss isn't used to being defied."

"Demanding, huh?"

"Sometimes," I admitted. "But she's fair. And I love my job."

"You like living and working in the city."

"Yes. I'm a city girl, through and through."

He pursed his mouth. "Where's your family?"

"There's just my dad," I said as casually as possible. "He lives in Boston. He's a criminal attorney, and he's extremely busy. I don't see him very often."

"Oh." He was polite enough not to press.

"How about your family?"

"My folks live about an hour north of me, and my brother lives in Albany. We're all close." He laughed. "Sometimes *too* close."

Envy struck me hard, and I realized that the more we talked, the more our differences were underlined. It was probably a good thing we hadn't exchanged many words last night, else we would've scared each other off before making it to bed. Jacki's ground rules were making more and more sense.

"There you are," April said, sashaying into view. She'd taken advantage of the break to freshen up. Her dark hair lay in perfect waves around her shoulders, and her lips were vibrant red. Sex appeal buffeted from her. "I'm starving," she said, then looked at Sam and licked her lips.

"Then we'll hurry," I said. "We wouldn't want you to wither away." I stabbed the elevator button, embarrassed for April for flirting, and embarrassed for me for caring that she flirted.

Throughout lunch, Sam seemed infuriatingly unaware of April's sucking-up. He laughed at her lame jokes and didn't object when she snitched a forkful of his rice pilaf. My head and nose were thoroughly stopped up by now, so I couldn't taste anything. Besides, I couldn't stop sneezing long enough to eat. I sat with my face in a hanky and watched April and Sam...relate. The longer I watched them, the more defrauded I felt. Sam was an equal-opportunity charmer. The connection I'd imagined last night was a byproduct of my naiveté. My former naiveté, I thought, remembering my newfound maturity.

I couldn't explain why it so bothered me that I'd been deluded—it wasn't as if Sam and I could ever have made a go of it. He lived in a small town; I lived in a small apartment. He drove a pickup; I'd driven twice. He had a big wholesome family, I had a big account with Thai-to-Go. And wasn't my body's rejection of him proof that Sam was all wrong for me?

Not soon enough, lunch ended. Sam was going straight to the airport, so he stepped to the curb to hail a taxi.

"If you're ever near Jar Hollow," he said to no one in particular, "look me up."

"Do you think you'll be back in the city any time soon?" April asked, her voice full of invitation.

He gave us a little smile, and shook his head. "I'm not much of a city boy."

My heart sagged. Translation: *There isn't anything worth coming back for.*

"It was very nice to meet you, Sam," April said, then offered her hand, palm down in case, I surmised, he wanted to kiss it. Instead he shook her hand and said something nice.

When he looked my way, I conjured up a cheerful smile. "I know all of Jar Hollow will be proud when the hometown hero issue is released in two weeks." I stuck out my hand. "Good luck."

He looked at my hand, then squeezed it between both of his hands. "Good luck to you, too, Kenzie." He winked, then swung into the cab. And just like that, my one-night stand rode away.

I had to listen to April chatter about him all the way back to the office. By the time we alighted from the elevator, I was ready to strangle her with my purse strap.

"And that *body,*" April said with a groan. "Can you imagine what the man looks like without clothes?"

"I can imagine," I said with a flat smile. "See you later." I peeled off toward my office and when I arrived, fell into my desk chair. I just wanted the day to end so I could go home, take a long bath, and sort things through. I wanted to call Jacki, but right now I didn't have the energy. Besides, this turn of events necessitated a face-to-face, alcohol-laced tête-à-tête. Somehow I dragged myself through the rest of the afternoon without giving in to the urge to open my purse for a look-see at the dildo. There was time later to ogle—and *enjoy*—I told myself.

I delivered the circulation summary report when I returned Helena's jacket. She wasn't in her office, but her phone was ringing. I picked up the receiver. "*Personality* magazine, Helena Birch's office."

"Is Ms. Birch available?" asked a woman with a heavy accent. Italian? Middle-Eastern?

"No, but I'll take a message."

"This is Madame Blackworth returning her call."

I frowned at the woman's sales-y, drawn-out enunciation. "I'll give her the message."

"Thank you."

I returned the phone and scribbled a message on a notepad, then picked up a thick stack of files from the box on Helena's desk that read "Kenzie." I heaved a sigh—not only would I be working late, but the weekend looked iffy.

Around seven-thirty, I was massaging my neck and contemplating going home. At least my allergy symptoms had subsided, and my appetite had returned. Thai-to-Go was sounding good. At a rap on my door, I looked up to see Helena standing there, briefcase in hand. "Ready to call it a day?" she asked.

"Almost," I said, surprised by her uncharacteristic little visit. "After I retrieve a few jobs I sent to the laser printer."

"Anything I need to take home?"

I was dying for her to read the memo I'd written on my ideas for updating the magazine cover, but I didn't want to seem too eager. "Nothing that can't wait until Monday."

"Fine." Helena hesitated, then said, "I stopped by to say thank you, Kenzie, and well done."

I blinked. Helena had said "please" on Monday, and was now playing loose with "thank you"?

"You're welcome, Helena. What did I do?"

"Perhaps you should tell *me*. I just got off the phone with Dr. Long."

Panic blipped in my chest. "You did?"

"Yes. He said he had originally decided against letting us use one of the photographs we took for the cover, but that you had changed his mind."

"I did?"

"Apparently so. You must tell me what you did to make such an impression on the man. He seemed to have enjoyed his trip very much. In fact, he said that he felt as if he had left something of himself behind."

I glanced toward my bag where the "something" was tucked away and smirked inwardly over Sam's wicked sense of humor. Still, it was nice of him to make me look good in my boss's eyes—no doubt to soften his brush-off.

I smiled at my boss. "I'm glad you'll have the cover you wanted, Helena."

"Yes," she said in a faraway voice. "It will help."

"It will help what?"

But instead of answering, she turned to leave. "Have a nice weekend, Kenzie."

6

"Wow," Jacki said.

"Double wow," Denise said.

We looked at Cindy, who was silent.

"I think she's speechless," Jacki said.

"I've never seen anything like it," Cindy murmured, mesmerized.

I stared at the impressive homemade dildo, which was situated in the middle of my kitchen table on the closest thing I could find to a pedestal—an overturned silver candy dish. The girls and I sat around the table, eating the Hershey's Kisses that had once been in the candy dish and drinking merlot.

"I have to hand it to you, Kenzie," Jacki said. "You know how to pick a one-night stand."

"And to think he's a doctor to boot," Denise said dreamily.

"And he's a hero," Jacki added.

Cindy was still staring. "I've never seen anything like it."

Denise hummed her agreement, which was notable considering she always talked about how amazingly endowed her ex-husband was. "If I were judging, it would definitely win a blue ribbon."

"Maybe Best in Show," Jacki said, nodding. "I think you should seriously consider having it bronzed, Kenzie."

Raising her glass, Denise said with reverence, "To the Eagle Scout."

We clinked our glasses and drank in homage. I thought Sam would have been pleased with the observance. What man wouldn't?

Denise peeled another Kiss. "I only wish I could have seen your face when he walked into that meeting."

"That had to be a shocker," Jacki said.

Cindy sighed. "I think it's the most romantic thing I've ever heard."

"Until the part where you broke out in hives," Denise said.

"And spilled coffee on his shirt," Jacki added.

"You haven't heard from him?" Cindy asked.

I shook my head, then popped two chocolate Kisses in my mouth and took a drink of wine, holding my tongue against the roof of my mouth until the rich tastes mingled. I swallowed. "And I don't expect to."

"It's only been two days," Jacki said. "And he doesn't have your home number, does he?"

"I didn't give it to him." Not that he'd asked.

"See? If he's going to call you, he'll call you at work tomorrow. Or sometime this week."

"Even if he did call, I'm allergic to the man, remember?"

Jacki pshawed. "That's baloney."

"I didn't make up the hives," I said. "Or the stuffy nose, or the sneezing."

"You're probably allergic to his cologne."

"He wasn't wearing any."

"Well, maybe it was his body lotion. Or, he's a veterinarian—maybe he had pet dander on his clothes."

That I couldn't argue with, but I had plenty of other ammunition. "Okay, *even if* he called, and *even if* my allergies magically disappeared, the man is a country doctor, and the last time I looked, I live in Manhattan."

"It worked on 'Green Acres,'" Cindy offered.

I ignored her. "Besides, Sam seemed very content being

single. And who knows, he might have a girlfriend in Mayberry that he forgot to mention." Not that I'd asked.

Jacki lifted her hands. "Your point?"

I frowned. "My point is that I am no longer willing to invest in men who aren't willing to invest in me."

"That's fair," Jacki agreed.

"And you're still convinced," Denise said, "that this man allergy is a natural defense mechanism to keep you away from bad boys?"

"Yes," I said primly. "My body will instinctively know a good fit when I find him."

Jacki sent a strange little smile my way. "Maybe so. Just remember your heart is part of your body, too."

THE NEXT MORNING, I sat down at my desk and tried to stir up some enthusiasm for the day's activities, which promised to be less than electrifying. The memory of Sam seemed to fill the cramped room—I tingled all over again when I remembered how he'd said he could get used to having me around. Of course I'd misunderstood what he'd meant.

On my Palm Pilot I called up my to-do list for the day and was faced with "Start looking for a nice guy."

I had placed a number 1 next to the item, indicating highest priority. Now, how to go about it?

My phone interrupted my thoughts, ringing with the single bleep of an external phone call. I stared at the receiver, rebelling against the hope that it was Sam calling. Why would Sam be calling me? No reason whatsoever.

I picked up the receiver on the third ring, hating the rapid beat of my heart and the breathless way I said, "Kenzie Mansfield."

"Hi, sweetheart. How's my girl?"

I smiled into the phone. "Hi, Dad. I'm fine."

"Good, good. I, uh, didn't want you to think I'd forgotten your birthday on Friday." His laugh boomed over the phone.

I bit into my lip. "It was Thursday, Dad. But that's okay."

"Thursday, right. I was traveling on business, sweetheart, and I couldn't break away to call you, but I was thinking about you."

Translation: He got into the office this morning and his secretary reminded him he'd missed my birthday. "Thanks, Dad," I said as cheerfully as I could manage.

"Why don't I come up on the train and we'll have lunch or dinner one day this week?"

I brightened. "How about Wednesday?"

"Hmm. I'll have Vanessa check my schedule, and I'll get back to you, okay?"

Same old, same old. "Fine, Dad. Just let me know when is good for you."

"I will, sweetheart. And be looking for something from me to arrive. Happy birthday."

"Thanks, Dad. Talk to you soon."

I hung up the phone, setting aside my own disappointment and thinking instead how disappointed Mom would be if she could see how my dad had disassociated himself from his only daughter. I couldn't be angry with my dad, though, because I knew how much he missed my mother, and how much being around me reminded him that our family was incomplete. He'd moved to Boston to escape the memories. These days, Christmas Eve was our only planned time together. I always rode the train to Boston for Father's Day unless he had other plans. And he usually managed to come up a couple of times during the year to have dinner or to see a show. Our arrangement wasn't the stuff that greeting card commercials were made of, but it was pleasant, and it was what it was.

Besides, Dad probably had thought by now I'd be married and he'd be off the hook as the main man in my life.

Which led me back to the high priority item on my to-do list. I decided, however, that the quest for a nice guy could wait at least until after my second helping of coffee, and trudged toward the break room to refill the Starbucks cup I'd bought and drained on my morning commute.

Surprised that Helena hadn't yet called me for our regular morning brief, I stopped by her office to see if I could bring her a cup of coffee. Her door was open, but she was on the phone, sitting behind her desk with her back turned. I frowned because I knew Helena better than anyone, and her body language was all wrong—closed, agitated. I hoped it wasn't bad news, and went on my way.

I pushed open the door to the break room to see April arched in a full-body yawn like a cat in heat. She gave me a fake smile as she lowered her arms. "Good morning, Kenzie."

"Good morning, April. How are you?"

"I'm fabulous," she said, then leaned her liberal hips against the counter and blew on the top of her coffee. "Sam called me."

I froze. "Excuse me?"

"*Sam* called me. You, know—Dr. Long."

The word *flummoxed* wasn't alien to me, but I had to admit that I'd never fully appreciated the emotion until that moment. I was flummoxed, but good. "*Sam* called you?" I repeated liked an idiot.

She smiled into her cup. "Uh-huh. Just a few minutes ago, in fact."

I knew I'd hate myself for asking, but I had to. "What did he want?"

She lifted her lovely shoulders in a shrug. "I couldn't say for sure, but he did mention what a nice time he'd had on Friday." She walked toward the door, her mug smug. "Have a nice day."

I watched her sashay away, then poured my coffee with a less-than-steady hand, furious at myself for letting anything that Sam Long did get to me. I'd gotten what I wanted out of the one-night stand, and so had he. End of story.

So why was I near tears? Because I'd projected a fantasy onto him to justify jumping into bed with a stranger? Because my dad had forgotten my birthday? Because the milk carton in the mini-fridge was empty—again?

I sipped from my coffee cup and scalded my tongue, bringing the tears to the surface. I was contemplating crawling into one of the cabinets for a good therapeutic cry when the door to the break room swung open. I turned to see Helena standing there, her face drawn. "Kenzie—I need the directors in meeting room A in ten minutes." She hesitated, then added, "And you too."

Helena pivoted and strode away before I could ask any questions, but dread settled in my stomach. My boss had never called an impromptu meeting to deliver *good* news.

As I hurried from office to office delivering the edict, my mind raced, mentally rechecking the previous week's to-do list. Had an important deadline been missed? A fact gone unverified? A dirty place-holding word inadvertently been left in an ad? (It happens.) Nothing sprang to mind, which worried me even more. Helena depended on me to anticipate problems, and obviously I'd mis-anticipated something.

I grabbed paper and pen and, sloshing coffee, I slipped into the meeting room, packed with nervous-looking colleagues. All seats were taken except for Helena's at the head of the table, which sat empty. Since chivalry had died in Manhattan in the forties, I leaned against the wall. A few seconds later a man I'd never seen before walked in and joined me on the wall.

"Daniel Cruz," he said, sticking out his hand. "I'm the new director of sales."

Early forties, nice face and voice. I introduced myself and shook his right hand while checking the other hand for a ring. Nada. I tensed for an allergic reaction, but my body seemed unaffected. He didn't strike me as being gay, but who knew these days. It could be that I was loaded with so much antihistamine that his pheromones had been rendered powerless.

"I hope we're not all going to be fired," he whispered, chuckling.

That paralyzing thought hadn't crossed my mind, but when Helena marched into the room with that wrinkle between her eyebrows, fear blipped in my chest that chuckling Daniel Cruz could be right. My search for a nice guy instantly became a lesser priority as I tried to recall if I'd seen a Help Wanted sign at Starbucks this morning.

Helena sought me out for a special look. Guilt? Remorse? I busied myself readying my paper and pen for note-taking, but my hands were sweaty. Helena took her place at the head of the table and everyone quieted.

"I'm going to cut to the chase," Helena said, then paused, as if she were struggling with what she had to say.

I'd never seen my boss at a loss for words, so my anxiety ratcheted up a notch while my imagination ran wild. *Our financing has dried up. Our number-one advertiser has pulled their business. We've been slapped with a lawsuit that involves every employee and not only are we all fired but our personal assets will be seized.* I held my breath, steeling myself for the worst.

"It appears," Helena finally said, "that our magazine has fallen under a cover curse."

And just like that, my life moved from unreal to *sur*real.

7

AS THE SILENCE in the boardroom dragged on, I hoped I had misunderstood what my boss had just announced. *A cover curse?*

Helena's strength as editor-in-chief rested in her unorthodox thinking, but recently she had become involved in all kinds of metaphysical mumbo jumbo in an attempt to ward off menopause. I'd grown accustomed to her spontaneous crystal rubbing, cross-legged meditation breaks, and occasional tribal screams. In fact, I suspected it was my pragmatic take on things that Helena most depended upon to maintain her balance. But I had a sudden fear that while I'd been immersed in my little personal drama the past few days, Helena had gone off the deep end of the New Age pool.

"A cover curse?" Daniel Cruz muttered. Tittering sounded, but Helena's stare restored quiet.

I wish I could say her stare also restored confidence, but I could tell my boss was coming unwound—her T-zone was shiny.

Helena wet her lips. "I should have said *there is a rumor* that the magazine has fallen under a cover curse." A shaky laugh escaped her. "Of course we're not under an actual curse—that would be absurd." She laughed again, the sound just as unconvincing as the first, and when it petered out, she looked lost.

Loyalty ballooned in my chest, and I felt compelled to

save her. "Helena, why would someone start such a ridiculous rumor?"

She gave me a grateful look, and seemed to reorient herself. She opened a folder and fanned three issues of *Personality* on the table. "The people on the covers of the last three issues have all been involved in freak accidents that occurred while their respective issue was on the stands."

Helena held up the issue featuring a supermodel-turned-humanitarian. "Some kind of space debris fell through the roof of Mia Compton's house and hit her." Next she held up the issue featuring a famous chef who had just launched his own line of gourmet foods. "Keith Kellor slipped on an orange juice spill in a grocery and is in traction." The third issue—last week's—featured a popular network news anchor. "And finally, Tara Duncan was electrically shocked by a faulty microphone."

Helena looked all around. "The injuries haven't been serious, thank goodness. Apparently Ms. Duncan had heard about Mr. Kellor's accident the previous week, and when the paramedics arrived, she made a crack that our magazine must have a cover curse."

"Seems harmless enough," Daniel Cruz offered from the wall.

Helena turned our way, glanced back and forth between the two of us as if we were in cahoots, then pursed her mouth. "For now, maybe. But I'm sure you can appreciate the fact that this isn't the kind of thing I want the magazine to be known for."

Daniel Cruz nodded, but he seemed to be fighting a smile. "So how is the person on this week's cover faring?"

Helena's mouth tightened at his flip tone and I inched away lest I be lumped in with the troublemaker. "I phoned Jane Suttles this morning," my boss said, "under the guise of another request, and she seems to be fine."

"She's the lady who sells cars and wears the jacket made of dollar bills?"

Helena nodded. "The top car salesperson in the country."

Daniel gave a dismissive wave. "Don't worry—you couldn't kill a car salesman if you tried."

Everyone laughed except Helena. And me, chicken that I was.

Daniel straightened in an apparent attempt to redeem himself. "If Jane Suttles is okay, then what's the problem?"

Helena frowned outright. "The *problem*, Mr. Cruz, is that today is only Monday. The Suttles issue will be on the stands until Sunday, when it will be replaced by the hometown hero issue."

Sam's issue—my heart blipped.

"Mind you," Helena said to everyone, "I don't expect anything to happen to Jane Suttles between now and Sunday." She reached up to massage her temple. "And even if something did happen, God forbid, it certainly wouldn't be because of this so-called curse." Her voice was starting to sound a little desperate. "But...I wanted to brief you in case *Variety* or a tabloid rag contacts you, or in case a subordinate asks questions. I want this rumor nipped in the bud, is that clear?"

Everyone nodded like the servants we were.

"Meanwhile," she said, her laser eyes slicing across the room, "not a *word* of what I said leaves this room."

More nodding ensued. I was glad I hadn't taken any notes else I might've had to eat them.

"That's all," Helena said, dismissing us.

I turned to leave.

"Kenzie, a moment please?"

I stopped and turned back. "Of course, Helena."

The furrow in Helena's brow concerned me. She waited

until everyone had left the room before she spoke. "Kenzie, is there anything you'd like to talk to me about?"

Panic spiked until I realized that I had no idea what she was talking about. "I don't think so."

She shifted in her chair. "I anticipate a very busy week so I'll have to ask you to postpone any lunch plans or appointments you might have."

My dad's possible visit came to mind. "Well, there's one potential—" When Helena's eyes clouded, I decided that the off chance of him coming wasn't worth getting her upset about. "Never mind," I said. "I'm available all week." Twenty-four-seven. It wasn't like anyone else was clamoring for my time.

"Good," she said. "I looked over the memo you wrote about the cover ideas. Very nice. I didn't realize you had such a flair for expressing yourself."

She was accustomed to me transcribing *her* thoughts. "Thank you. I keep thinking I might do something with my journalism degree someday."

Helena paled, and I realized how she might have misunderstood. "I mean, working for you has been a wonderful experience."

Her mouth twitched. "But?"

But nothing...although I recognized an opening when I saw one. "But...I'd like to try my hand at writing filler pieces." I swallowed. "Occasionally." I shifted. "If that would be okay with you."

I waited for her to say that she was only flattering me, that my writing wasn't up to par to write for *her* magazine, and, in truth, I would've preferred that she say it than think it and not say it. But deep down I yearned for Helena to say that my writing *was* good enough, and that she'd be proud to have my byline in her magazine.

"I'll keep your offer in mind, Kenzie," she said finally. "In the meantime, let's get through this week."

I nodded.

When I got back to my office, a huge vase of white lilies sat on my desk. I smiled—Vanessa must have told my dad that missing my birthday necessitated something more special than the roses he sent every year. They *were* lovely. I pulled out the card and read the requisite Happy Belated Birthday! and allowed myself a single bittersweet pang of...loss? wistfulness? before removing the vase to the hall so I'd have room to turn around. When I sat back down at my desk, I pushed my hands into my hair and took a deep breath, thinking about all the news I had yet to absorb.

I had shared my writing aspirations with Helena, surprising myself. Surprise, I decided, was good for the soul.

I wasn't sure what to make of this cover curse thing, only that I hoped it died down before Sam's issue hit the stands. Since he hadn't been keen on being on the cover in the first place, I'd hate to see him sucked into a vortex of unwanted publicity.

And Sam had called April. That smarted, I had to admit. Still, knowing that he was the kind of guy who would call April only reinforced my opinion that I was mistaken in my favorable estimation of the man. A half hour later when I found myself still thinking about him, I realized if I was going to get through this busy week, I would have to purge Dr. Sam Long from my mind.

I succeeded, for the most part. As Helena promised, I had plenty of work to keep me occupied, and then some. In fact, I had the faint impression that Helena was intentionally burying me in work, which did not give me warm fuzzies for having asserted my opinions. Maybe it was just in my mind, but it seemed that some invisible wall had sprung up between us—Helena withdrew into her office and we communicated by cryptic phone and e-mail messages, and through passed file folders. I tried to blame her mood on hot flashes, but I confess that I took it personally and I could feel myself pulling back as well. Monday and Tuesday passed in a paperwork haze.

Wednesday, however, brought a couple of developments in my life. One I'd anticipated, but the other was a bona fide *gotcha.*

Dad's secretary called to say he couldn't make it up to see me that week, but would try to catch up with me the following week. Nothing new there.

And Daniel Cruz called and asked me to go to the movies with him. Saturday. Eight o'clock. A romantic comedy. He'd pick me up. I was stunned. I said yes.

By the time Friday afternoon rolled around, I was sure the long hours over my desk would result in a humped back, but I wasn't too worried because I was starting to think I might actually be settled down with a nice guy before the hump became too unsightly.

And, I was happy to say, Dr. Sam Long was receding in my thoughts.

Okay, only a little. But it was a start.

At five minutes until five o'clock, my phone rang. It was Helena.

"Kenzie, could you come to my office, please?"

At the somber tone of her voice, I knew something was up. I only hoped, as I walked to her office, that it wasn't my employment contract. She probably had noticed the wall that had sprung up between us and wanted to replace me. Admittedly I *had* been operating all week in a fog, distracted by personal events and non-events. She probably thought I was so taken with the idea of writing for the magazine that I'd lost focus on her objectives. Mentally rehearsing an apology, I knocked on Helena's office door.

"Come in."

I opened the door and walked in. Helena still had that pinched looked. "Close the door, Kenzie."

I obliged, then wobbled to one of the chairs sitting in front of her desk and sat on the edge.

Helena steepled her hands in front of her and sighed. I was on the verge of throwing myself at her feet when she spoke.

"Kenzie, I have a special assignment, and I think you're the best person for it."

I blinked. "Okay." Then I remembered the "assignment" involving the pet salon. "Is this work-related?"

Helena seemed distracted. "Hmm? Oh, yes." She sighed again and worked her mouth from side to side. "Kenzie, what do you make of this cover curse business?"

"I...don't believe in curses. The freak accidents are all just a coincidence."

Helena nodded, then sighed again. "I just received word that Jane Suttles fell off a platform where she was staging an event and broke both arms."

My hand flew to my throat. "That's terrible."

"For her and for us. The accident will only fuel the fire if word of this silly cover curse gets out. So you'll understand why I'm asking you to do what I'm going to ask you to do."

I waited.

"I've arranged for you to visit Dr. Long in Jar Hollow for a few days."

My heart sputtered. "Excuse me?"

"The issue with his picture on the cover will hit the stands Sunday. For the week that he'll be on the cover, I need someone to keep an eye on him."

"Keep an eye on him?" I squeaked.

She nodded. "Part baby-sitter, part bodyguard. You're perfect for the job."

"I'm perfect for the job?" My vocabulary had vanished. I could only repeat what was being said to me.

"Absolutely. Dr. Long knows you and seems to enjoy your company. I've taken the liberty of calling him. I told him you were coming to write an article on the life of a small-town veterinarian."

"Write an article?"

"You said you wanted to try your hand at writing."

"Try my hand at writing."

Helena spread her hands. "Here's your chance. While you're there, all you have to do is keep Dr. Long out of trouble."

"Out of trouble?"

"Keep him so busy playing host and taking you on house calls or barn calls or whatever he does that he doesn't have time to run around putting out fires and being in danger."

"Helena, I can't stop the man from responding to a fire!"

"Well if you can't distract him, at least you'll be able to let me know if something happens before anyone else finds out. Then we can organize damage control if we have to."

"How will I get there?"

"You do drive, don't you?"

"In the loosest sense of the word."

She dismissed my concern with a wave. "You'll be fine."

"Where will I stay?"

"Dr. Long has guest quarters."

"At his home?" I was weak—or giddy, I couldn't be sure. "When would I leave?"

"Tomorrow morning. You should arrange for a rental car to be delivered to your flat."

"H-how long would I stay?"

"Until next Sunday, when the new issue will hit the stands." She shoved a folder into my hands. "I've made some notes to help you with the article. Stay in touch."

My head felt as if it might explode. I was supposed to show up on Sam's doorstep and play house with the man for a week? I had to sit down. When I realized I was already sitting down, I considered sprawling on the floor.

"Oh, and Kenzie—there is one other thing."

I swallowed, thinking there was nothing she could say to make things worse.

"I've been thinking about Dr. Long's recommendation to have Angel spayed, and I decided he's right. He'll be expecting her."

"Expecting her?" I was back to repeating.

Helena cleared her throat. "Dr. Long agreed to spay Angel this week."

Dread settled in my stomach. "And how exactly is Angel supposed to *get* to Dr. Long's?"

My boss angled her head and gave me a magnanimous smile. I realized that things could indeed be worse.

8

"CALL ME when you get there," Helena said. She threw Angel a kiss, and waved until we disappeared from sight in the silver Volvo I'd rented (a safe car, I'd justified). Right away, Angel, who sported a floppy lavender bow between her ears and sat on a pink blanket in the passenger seat, began to whine.

"I know how you feel," I said, nursing nausea over the thought of seeing Sam again, and under such convoluted circumstances.

Angel gave me a doubting look.

"Okay, so I'm not going to have to get *fixed* when I get there," I conceded, "but trust me—it's for your own good. When you leave, you'll be cured of the male element altogether, while I..." I swallowed hard. "Won't be."

Angel wasn't buying it. She must have sensed my perverted feeling of relief that having her doomed little uterus along lent more credibility to my trip. It wasn't as if Sam had *invited* me to travel upstate and observe him offering up cures for spoon-swallowing pigs for this article I was writing. Despite that Helena had contacted him to set up this excursion before she even told me about it, I was paranoid that he'd think it was my idea in a desperate attempt to get close to him.

Granted, during the three-minute conversation I'd had with him last night, he hadn't sounded suspicious or perturbed about having me and Angel as houseguests for the next week, but I chalked up his cheerfulness to country manners. Besides directions, the only extra conversation he'd offered was, "Bring a pair of boots." I wasn't completely clear why, but I'd dutifully packed my red calfskin Stuart Weitzman boots along with enough antihistamine to spike pharmaceutical stock prices. At the last minute, I added the homemade dildo. Since Sam had agreed to cast the mold when he thought he'd never see me again, I thought it only fitting to return it.

That wasn't a conversation I wanted to think about.

For the drive I had opted for a pair of black Seven corduroy slacks, a pale yellow Juicy Couture sweater, and a pair of teal, mid-heel Miss Sixty slides. I'd dressed down because, assuming that life in Jar Hollow was a bit more casual than Manhattan, I didn't want to stand out from the locals.

I tried to force aside my concerns about my destination and concentrate on the matter at hand: driving. I could count on one hand the times I'd sat behind a steering wheel, and the instrument panels of cars had changed quite a bit in the fifteen years since I'd passed my driving exam in the coned-off parking lot of the DMV.

After much trial and error, I found a pop rock station on the radio, then turned the shiny Volvo in a northwesterly direction and settled in for the four-hour drive.

One hour in, the skyline had disappeared behind me, I was tired of pop rock, and we had encountered a particularly curvy two-lane road. Angel's head began to bounce like a bobble-head doll, then she started projectile vomiting. *Carsickness,* I deduced rather quickly.

By the time I'd guided the car onto the shoulder of the road, I was gagging, and would have upchucked myself if I'd had breakfast. I stuffed bits of paper napkin up my nose to ward off the stench, then tackled the mess with more napkins and a bottle of pricey spring water. By the time I got Angel and her surroundings cleaned up, I was seriously considering turning around and hightailing it back to NYC.

My cell phone rang. I dug it out of the depths of my shoulder bag, praying it was Helena calling the whole thing off. "Hello?"

"How's it going?" Jacki asked.

I laid my head back. "Badly. Both the dog and I are carsick. I think it's a sign."

"It doesn't take much to get you sick," Jacki pointed out. "Besides, you're on your way to see a doctor, right? He'll make you all better when you get there."

"Since I'm not imposing enough as it is."

"Hey, this wasn't your idea."

I chewed on my tongue, then voiced the concern that had been niggling at the back of my mind from the get-go. "I could have said no."

"Yes."

"Well."

"Well, what?"

"Well, what do you suppose that means?" I demanded.

"Hmm, let's see—you didn't say no to spending a week in the country with a gorgeous doctor who has a yonker the size of a summer sausage? I believe that means you're not insane."

"You know I can't *do* anything with him while I'm there," I hissed. "I'm going on business, and the man has a heart problem. I'm supposed to look out for him, not incite a coronary." (In a desperate moment, I had divulged the cover curse rumor to Jacki, with the promise of a slow death if she told anyone.)

"He seemed to have survived your first night together."

I thought about April's assertion that the good doctor

wouldn't last long in her company, and realized that my being the least likely person to mix business with pleasure was probably one of the reasons I got this assignment. "I'm not going to press my luck."

"Come on—do you really believe you can live under the same roof with the man for a week and not give in to temptation?"

"Jacki, this will be different from meeting in a dark bar. We know each other now."

"All the better."

I shook my head at her romanticism. "Even if Sam wanted to...you know—and I don't believe he will—I can't risk it."

"Can't risk what?"

"My *job,*" I said. "Remember—that little thing I call a career? And I can't risk my health, either. I'm allergic, remember?"

"Yeah, I remember," Jacki said, her voice thick with frustration. "I have to run."

"Are you and Ted doing something this weekend?" A dumb question considering they were spending almost every spare moment together.

"We're driving to the Jersey shore for the day."

"Sounds fun," I mumbled. "When will I get to meet this guy?"

"When you cut the cord between you and Helena Birch. You work too much."

"Easy for you to say, Jacki—you're a success in your field. But I feel like I'm so...behind. Overdue. If this is my big break, I want to make the most of it."

Jacki sighed. "Then go for it. But wear your seatbelt. And give yourself permission to have a good time. And call me."

"Okay." I slowly disconnected the call and looked over

at Angel. The pooch sagged against the seat, but at least the sparkle had returned to her beady little eyes.

For some reason I didn't want to explore too deeply, her beady little eyes reminded me of Daniel Cruz. "I reneged on a date with a perfectly nice guy to go on this road trip," I informed my traveling companion.

Angel lifted her head and yipped, as if encouraging me to go back.

I spied a lone quarter in the plastic console between us. "Coin toss," I announced. "Heads we go forward, tails we go back."

Angel seemed agreeable.

I tossed the coin in the air, but my eye-hand coordination wasn't the best. (Okay, I was always the kid who took score during recess sports.) I missed, and the quarter fell down the crack between my seat and the console. Angel looked at me and I pursed my mouth, trying to decide what I'd wanted the coin to tell me.

God help me, I did want to see Sam again, if only to put to rest the perception that I was a tipsy, shirt-snatching woman who made a habit out of picking up guys at bars for one-night stands.

"Okay, we can do this," I said. "We'll go and make the best of it. What's the worst that can happen?"

Angel gave me the dubious look of someone about to go under the knife, which I decided to ignore. But when the faint scent of throw-up reached my nose, I realized that in order for the remainder of the drive to be tolerable, we'd need to roll down the windows. Since the spring temps were still a bit chilly, I pulled an Amy Tangerine coat from my suitcase, and opened the Louis Vuitton overnight case that Helena had given me for Angel. From the jaw-dropping array of sweaters, coats, collars, accessories and food treats that looked good enough for human consumption, I found a lavender polka-dot sweater (designer) to match the bow in her hair. I had never dressed a dog before, so that took a little maneuvering, but in the end, Angel looked every inch the princess that she was. The pooch seemed to know she was color-coordinated because she perked up a bit, even licked my face a couple of times. I was glad I had packed anti-bacterial sanitizer.

I rolled down my window, but lowered the passenger-side window only a couple of inches to circumvent potential disasters in the event Angel had suicidal tendencies. Still, the ventilation was enough to send the wind whipping through the car like a whirlwind when we got under way. I turned up the radio volume and we sped down the highway like a couple of girls resigned to whatever fate flung our way.

We drove by and through numerous towns. Since I rarely left the city, I found the foliage and the signage positively fascinating—people put words on anything that didn't move, including roofs and water towers. The farther I drove, the more quaint the names of the towns. Tree Gum. Weeping Wonder. Used Branch. (Used for what, I was dying to know.)

I wasn't making good time because after nearly going airborne when I swerved to miss what might have been a squirrel, I had driven the last one hundred miles with one foot on the gas and one on the brake in case any other critters decided to hurl themselves underneath my wheels.

Okay...I'd also taken a couple of wrong turns and mistakenly zoomed through a rest area going fifty miles an hour, but only because the directions I'd downloaded from the Internet weren't as clear as they could have been. Suffice it to say that when I saw the sign that promised Jar Hollow, 4 miles, I was enormously relieved. And I was, according to the ETA I'd given Sam, about three hours late.

I'd lost the signal to my cell phone a few minutes after saying sayonara to Jacki, and both of the pay phones at my last pit stop had been amputated at the cord. It was good to know that vandalism wasn't confined to the city.

I rolled into the city limits of Jar Hollow, population 5,842 at 7:00 p.m. with a full bladder and shin splints from toggling the foot pedals. Despite the ventilation, I suspected I reeked of doggie throw-up, so I thought it prudent to freshen up before I saw Sam again. I also needed directions to his residence because the page with that information had been sucked out the window during the squirrel incident.

Jar Hollow was a picturesque little town, complete with a town square populated by a few pipe-smoking old men, a bubbling fountain and a waving American flag. Yellow tulips marched along the base of a monument holding a cannon. I looked for a barber-shop pole and found it on the other side of the square—Doo-Dad's was open for business. A few doors down, Fi's Flowers was having a sale on carnations, and farther down the street, a red-and-white striped awning marked an ice cream shop, the word *Malts* spelled out in neon. I'd never had a malt, but assumed they were pretty good to warrant that kind of window space.

The downtown area consisted of about ten blocks of squatty brown brick buildings with long, large windows, some empty, some claimed by a community college extension program. All I could think was how much and how quickly they would go in the city as loft apartments or condos. The downtown area seemed to be situated on the lowest-lying land in the city. Tree-covered hills hemmed the town, then gave way to tree-covered plateaus dotted with house roofs and ribbons of roads. The lime-green of new spring growth swathed every living thing. I was in a Norman Rockwell painting. Me and my purple-sweatered dog.

A few hundred feet ahead I spotted a place called Chickle's, which appeared to be a diner with gas pumps and a souvenir shop that sold gen-u-wine Indian arrowheads. And most importantly, Chickle's looked as if it probably had indoor bathrooms—a must since the clerk at the last place I'd stopped had handed me a key with a wooden paddle attached to it and pointed "around back."

I parked the Volvo, scooped up my purse and Angel, and entered the establishment, which was relatively busy and smelled like French fries. A balding man behind the cash register shouted, "Hi there, how are you?"

"Fine," I said, then remembered my manners. "How are you?"

He beamed. "If I was any better, you'd have to buy me!"

I blinked.

"Stop flirting, Hap." A rusty-haired woman in a smock sidled up and shook her head. "Excuse my husband, miss. He hasn't looked in a mirror in twenty years." The woman smiled. "Cute dog."

"She's not mine," I said, "but thanks. Is it all right to have her in here?"

The woman nodded. "The health inspector is married to my sister."

Fair enough. "Do either of you know Dr. Sam Long?"

Hap nodded. "Pert near everyone around here knows the doc. Is your dog sick?"

"She's not mine," I repeated. "But no. I'm a writer here to do a story on Dr. Long, and I lost the directions to his place."

The woman's face lit up. "Does this have anything to do with the doc being on the cover of *Personal* magazine?"

"*Personality*," I corrected. "Yes, I work for the magazine. I'm doing a...follow-up piece."

She wore the adoring expression of a mother. "We're so proud of Doc Long. My great-aunt Maida was one of the folks he saved from the fire."

"That's wonderful."

She nodded, then her expression turned suspicious. "Is the doc expecting you?"

"Yes." Angel yipped. "Both of us," I corrected.

"Did you just drive up from the city?"

"I did."

"You're a long way from home," Hap said.

Not really, but I knew what he meant. I was also a little concerned that he could tell I was a city girl, although I decided that assessment might have something to do with the fact that I was holding a clothed dog.

"Are you staying with the doc?" he asked.

"Enough, Hap," the wife said, giving him a shove. "You know Doc Long has guest quarters over his office." She turned back to me and smiled. "We have a temperamental parakeet that we've taken out to see the doc a time or two. Have you had supper yet?"

"Supper? Um, no."

"Then my guess is you'll need to grab a bite to eat in town before you head out to his place anyway. And since it'll be dark soon, the doc will probably want to meet you so you don't have to drive on that road alone."

This was starting to sound ominous. "Is it far?"

"Not as the crow flies, but the doc lives in the boonies."

I had a general idea of what the boonies were, but I opted for clarification. "Pardon me?"

Hap grinned. "You know, the boonies—in the sticks. Off the beaten path."

"Don't worry," the woman said with a laugh. "There's indoor plumbing."

"Ah. May I use your phone?"

"To call the doc?"

I was actually considering calling Helena to tender my resignation, but I nodded.

"No need," the woman said, looking beyond my shoulder. "I do believe Sam's truck just pulled in. Looks like you're covered."

"Oh..." I conjured up a smile that belied my shaking insides. "Goody."

9

I REMEMBERED what Sam Long looked like, of course, but I had to admit I'd forgotten the impact of his brown, brown eyes on my green, green heart. And that grin...oh...*yeah.*

"Hi, Kenzie."

He was delectable looking in an army-green J Crew T-shirt (I knew T-shirts), and no-name jeans that fit him intimately. He wore low-heeled leather workboots of an indistinguishable color that were well acquainted with the outdoors, and it occurred to me that my high-heeled red boots might be in for some serious exposure to...country elements.

"Hello, Sam."

He looked as if he were considering the proper greeting for a one-night-stand-turned-business-associate. I was thinking handshake, arm squeeze or maybe a shoulder hug, but the kiss on the corner of my mouth really took me by surprise.

By the time I registered the warmth of his breath and the familiarity of his mouth on mine, the kiss was over. A few heartbeats later I realized, to my horror, that my eyes were still closed. I pried them open and found Sam smiling as if nothing was amiss. Hap and his wife's reaction was something more akin to mine, minus the sudden itch that assailed my neck. My man allergy appeared to be intact.

"I see you found us," Sam said. "I was on the verge of sending out a search party."

I was mildly pleased that he'd been worried. "You were?"

"Yeah, your boss called a half dozen times to see if you'd arrived."

Ah, Helena had been the worried one. "I lost cell phone service, and I ran into a couple of delays," I said, hedging, then decided to blame it all on Angel. "And you can't imagine how difficult it is to travel with an animal." When I remembered what he did for a living, I felt like an idiot. "Well, I guess *you* can imagine." I tried to laugh, thinking if I didn't get my act together, he'd never believe I was there to do an in-depth story on the life of a small-town vet. I cleared my throat. "How did you know I was here?"

"I thought I'd ride into town to see if anyone had seen you, and I spotted the car." He pointed with his thumb. "Not many silver Volvos with Manhattan tags in Jar Hollow. Nice ride."

"It's a rental. I don't own a car." Which sounded as if I was reminding him of our differences right up-front, in case he'd forgotten.

He shrugged amiably. "Guess you don't have much need for one."

An awkward silence ensued, during which I could think of nothing except how surreal this whole situation seemed. When we'd gone back to his hotel room that night and rolled around like the sex-starved strangers we were, neither one of us had expected this continuum. From the light flush on his cheeks, I thought he might be thinking the same thing.

Then again, he could be sunburned.

My travel companion broke the silence with a complaining little yip.

"And this must be Angel," Sam said.

The pooch perked up when she heard her name. I smirked. "Helena said you would be expecting her."

He nodded and scratched Angel behind her ear. "I'm going to fix pretty little Angel right up," he said with a wink. "We don't want her playing loose with the boys and getting into trouble."

I swallowed. "No, we don't want that." Mine was, of course, the voice of morality talking.

"I was hoping we'd have time to sit and eat dinner," he said, "but I just got a call about a family dog that was hit by a car."

"It wasn't me," I said quickly, wondering if the poor squirrel I'd brushed was lying in a ditch somewhere recovering.

One side of his mouth lifted. "I didn't think it was you."

"Um, are the injuries serious?"

"No, fortunately. A broken leg, but I'll take X-rays to rule out internal injuries. I told the Randalls to meet me at the clinic at home—do you mind if we get carryout?"

We...hmm. "Not at all."

He waved at Hap's wife. "Arma, can you get us a bucket of chicken to go?"

"Sure, doc—regular or extra crispy?"

He looked at me.

I assumed they weren't referring to a grilling method, and my familiarity with fried chicken was limited at best. But when in Rome... "Extra crispy."

Sam grinned, so I must have scored points. "Throw in some extra biscuits and gravy, Arma. I'm starving."

I was starving, too, but gravy still didn't sound appetizing. Come to think of it, I wasn't even sure I knew what gravy *was*.

"It'll be about fifteen minutes," Arma said, scuttling toward the diner side of the establishment and giving me a thorough once-over in the process. "Grab yourselves a seat."

Sam gestured toward a booth. When faced with the prospect of making small talk, I suddenly remembered my disheveled state and excused myself and Angel to the ladies' room to freshen up. It took me two minutes to powder my nose and scrutinize my blotchy neck in the hazy mirror over the sink. For the next thirteen minutes I stared at my watch and Angel stared at me.

"I know what you're thinking," I said. "You're thinking if I'm nervous about being alone with him in public for fifteen minutes, how am I going to get through this week?"

Angel tilted her head.

I moaned and leaned into the sink for support. "You're right," I wailed. "How am I going to get through this week?"

Seeing Sam again had hit me hard, and the scary part was that I didn't know why. Yet. Entirely. I had a sneaky suspicion that I wasn't ready to consider. I could admit, though, that I'd wanted to see him again, but he made me feel scared and clumsy and hungry. And the kiss had thrown me off.

I replayed the half kiss in my mind and tried to figure out what it had meant. Hello? Missed you? Did he kiss all the women he knew like that? Had he thought I expected it?

I touched my finger to my lower lip and studied my reflection. Big of eye and wide of nostril. Anxious. Confused. Allergic. And very, very out of place. I shouldn't have come—I had a bad feeling that before I escaped Jar Hollow I was going to have to suffer through more than a long-running case of the hives.

Then my gaze was drawn to a faded Keep on Truckin' sticker that had been affixed in who-knew-what decade in the lower left corner of the mirror. I had the eerie feeling that it had been put there for my benefit, for this very moment. I straightened. I could keep on truckin'.

As long as it didn't require having an actual truck, of course.

Then a light bulb flashed on in my head. I was allegedly here to get an article—if things became sticky or awkward between me and Sam, I'd simply go into interview mode. Fire questions, record answers, reestablish a professional distance.

There—I was brilliant.

Because even though the article was a cover, I was determined that this would be the best darned article ever written about a small-town veterinarian. I wasn't sure who or what was to blame for the sudden uneasiness between me and Helena—maybe she sensed my maternal attachment toward her and was trying to put professional distance between us. I had the smarts to realize that was probably a good thing, so scoring with this piece would be just the ticket to prove to Helena I was all business, and keeping an eye on Sam would show her that I was willing to go above and beyond the call of duty for the magazine. This trip, I decided, was a means to an end—the launch of my dream to write.

Jacki's words about resisting the temptation of Sam came back to me, and I realized that my man allergy might be my saving grace this week by helping me to keep my priorities straight. Resolve puffed out my chest—if I had to sacrifice my allergic body to male pheromones for the greater good, then so be it.

Of course, the half kiss notwithstanding, Sam Long might not be interested in picking up where we'd left off. If so, this week certainly would be easier than I'd planned.

I felt wetness on my foot and experienced a rush of

warmth toward Angel for licking me in my moment of need. Until I realized that she'd just taken a pee on my Miss Sixty's.

It was a sign that nothing in my life these days had any intention of getting easier.

When I emerged from the ladies' room, a line had formed. I gave the women apologetic looks and tried not to stare at their clothes even though they were staring at mine. And Angel's. Bulky ski sweaters, jeans and tennis shoes seemed to be the norm. I reasoned that the shopping choices in Jar Hollow were probably limited, and consoled myself that I didn't look too out of place.

"Who's the Barbie?" someone whispered loudly.

"Is she carrying a *dog?*" another woman said.

"Must be Big City Barbie," another added in a scathing voice.

My cheeks were burning when I approached Sam, who stood by the booth with one arm full of chicken and the other arm full of...chick.

The dark-skinned, lush-figured brunette reminded me of April Bromley, and from the proprietary way this woman touched Sam's arm, I had a feeling that I was looking at Sam's "type." Not to mention his girlfriend.

Sam did start guiltily when he saw me approach. I slowed my step, lest I overhear something personal. My heart was beating harshly even while I told myself that knowing he was attached only made things simpler. Act natural, I told myself. Just as if I hadn't been up close and personal with this woman's personal handhold.

"Kenzie Mansfield," Sam said, gesturing toward the gorgeous young woman. "Meet Val Jessum."

I conjured up my best don't-worry-he's-all-yours smile. "Pleased to meet you, Val. Will you be joining Dr. Long and me for dinner?"

I'd caught her off guard. Eyes that had been ready to sling arrows went wide and her gaze flew to Sam's. "Oh, well...I don't think so, not this time."

"Sometime before I leave then," I said easily.

"Sure," she murmured.

"Sorry to be in a rush," Sam said, "but I need to get to the clinic."

"See you later," Val said, looking back and forth between us.

I pushed open the door, partly because I was used to doing it for myself, and partly because I didn't want Sam looking too chivalrous around me with his girlfriend looking on.

"Sorry about that," Sam said, when we got outside.

"About what?" I asked, wide-eyed.

He hesitated a split second, then scratched his temple. "Never mind. Follow me—if we're separated by traffic, I'll pull onto the shoulder and wait."

Traffic? It was time for me to scratch *my* head. "Okay."

He climbed into a white double-cab pickup truck—April would be drooling—and I situated Angel in the passenger seat of the Volvo.

I'd be lying to myself if I said the appearance of a girlfriend hadn't shaken me. Did they have a commitment? And had he broken it by sleeping with me? I didn't want to think so, but it was none of my business. In truth, it seemed downright unrealistic to think that Sam *didn't* have a permanent woman in his life.

And I kept coming back to the question of why it should bother me—I had no claim on the man.

My mind was swirling as I opened the driver's-side door. The quarter I'd tossed poked out beneath the seat. Tails—we should have gone back. I curled my fingers around the coin and sighed. Too late now. I glanced to the left and Sam's grin through the open window made my heart jerk sideways.

Too late for a lot of things.

10

THE DRIVE to Sam's place took so long, I started to think maybe I should have brought the bucket of chicken with *me*—for a snack along the way. We didn't cover much ground, but the terrain was so rugged—and vertical—we were forced to travel at a snail's pace. Darkness was starting to fall, and the trees lining what passed for a road blocked out what little daylight was left. I was really getting creeped out, probably because I'd seen too many horror movies set in the woods.

Just before my ears started popping from the altitude, the ground leveled out, and the trees gave way to a clearing where two buildings sat about fifty yards apart. I stared at the larger building, and my heart fell to my stomach. "He lives in a log cabin?"

I looked down at Angel, who tilted her head.

"He *lives* in a log cabin," I repeated. I supposed the heavy feeling in my gut came from the realization that the sight before me clinched the differences between us—pint-sized apartment versus hand-hewn homestead. We might as well have lived on separate planets.

Sam parked his whopper truck between the two log buildings in a worn grassy area lit by a big globe on a telephone pole. I pulled my car into a spot next to him and climbed out gingerly.

"What do you think?" Sam asked, throwing his arm in the air toward...everything.

"It's really...something," I declared, circling in place. No matter what direction I turned, the scene was the same—trees. Tall and thick and unending, pressing upon us, hissing as the wind pushed them around. I longed for the comforting crush of skyscrapers and lights and street noise. Here the only sound was...whining.

I glanced toward the car and saw Angel standing with her nose pressed against the window. I jogged around to the passenger side and opened the door to let her out. But when I set her on the ground, she did a funny little dance, lifting her feet like a high-stepping show horse. She sniffed the packed ground suspiciously. It dawned on me that Angel had never before walked on dirt, and before I could snicker, I realized that the only time I had trod upon anything other than asphalt and grass was the time I'd happened upon water-line construction in Central Park.

I glanced at Sam and decided to keep the fact that I was a dirt virgin from the Eagle Scout. "Is that your clinic?" I asked, gesturing toward the smaller log building.

He nodded. "Want to see it? The Randalls are about ten minutes behind us, and I need to prep an exam room."

"That's why I'm here," I said cheerfully. "Let me grab my notebook and camera."

"You can call your boss from the phone in my office to let her know you arrived safely."

I did just that. Sam left me in his office, then disappeared down the hall, flipping on lights to the tune of much screeching and cage-rattling in other rooms. The hair raised on my arms just wondering what kinds of creatures he housed here. Angel, the more curious of the two of us, followed him and I let her, experiencing a surge of relief that someone else was looking after her for a few minutes. I turned and stared at the unbelievable chaos he called a work space, then stepped around stacks of books, files and paper to catch the trail of a phone line and follow it to a base unit sitting under a pile of mail. I recalled Sam's comment about his disorganization and vowed to remember his penchant for understatement.

I blew dust off the phone, then dialed Helena's number. She answered on the first ring.

"Kenzie?"

My chest tingled at the concern in her voice—maybe I'd imagined the recent distance between us. "Yes, Helena, it's me. I ran into a few delays, but I'm at Dr. Long's—"

"How is Angel?"

I smirked, thinking I should've known the concern was all for her dog. "She's fine, trying to adjust to dirt."

"Dirt?"

Apparently it was a foreign concept to Helena, too. "Um, she's fine."

"Does Dr. Long suspect why you're there?"

Her second concern—the magazine. I looked over my shoulder to make sure I was alone. "I don't think so."

"He hasn't said anything about the cover curse, has he?"

"No, but we haven't had much time to talk. He's preparing for a patient now."

"Tell me it isn't a big, dangerous animal, like a mountain lion."

I blinked—there were mountain lions in this area? "Uh, no, it's just a family dog."

"Good. Try to keep him from taking on anything too hazardous. And I've been thinking that someone might try to contact Dr. Long about the cover curse. Is there a way you can screen his calls?"

I frowned. "What? *No,* I can't screen his calls. And I don't know that it would be such a bad thing if he did find out—wouldn't he be more careful?"

"Kenzie," Helena chirped, "how would it look if everyone thought we actually believed in this cover curse enough to send someone to watch him?"

Something false and fearful in her voice stirred a memory chord...the woman with the exotic voice I'd taken a message from—Madame something-or-other. The only people who went by Madame these days were brothel keepers and *psychics*. Aha! "Helena, is there something you aren't telling me?"

"I don't know what you mean."

I wasn't comfortable confronting my boss about her phone conversations, so I tried another tack. "Helena, do *you* believe in this curse?"

"Kenzie, that would be...unnatural."

I pursed my mouth. She *so* believed in this curse. "Is that why you wanted Sam on the cover, because he's big and strong and less likely to come to harm?"

"Oh, there's my doorbell, Kenzie. I'm glad you and my Angel arrived safely. I'll check in with you tomorrow."

I hung up the phone feeling befuddled...and a little used. Helena hadn't been completely up-front with me, but then again, did her opinion of this cover curse really change my circumstances? Still, I had that panicky feeling of the situation spinning out of control. And deep down, I wondered what I would do if something did happen to Sam on my watch. And how I felt about the possibility of something happening to Sam, period—not good. I toyed with the idea of telling him about the cover curse.

"How's it going in here?"

I jumped and turned around, then my knees weakened. If possible, the man was even more breathtaking in a white lab coat. I didn't need the stethoscope hanging around his neck to know my heartbeat had picked up. I realized how ludicrous a cover curse would sound to him, and decided to stick with my original story—the article I was writing. "It's going...well."

He looked sheepish. "Sorry about the mess in here—I can never seem to catch up on my paperwork."

"Do you have an assistant?"

"Um, not at the moment." He glanced at his watch. "Are you starving?"

My mouth was watering, but not for fried chicken. "I'm fine."

"I hope this appointment won't take too long, then we can eat and relax."

Relax? There went my heart again. Was Sam expecting us to...you know? Somehow I had the feeling that Val Jessum wouldn't be too keen on the idea of Sam and me...relaxing. And I had made up my mind—if he tried anything like that confusing little half kiss again, I was going to have to set him straight.

From another room came a high-pitched screech, then Angel came skidding into view. Sam laughed and leaned over to pick her up.

"What was that?" I asked, not sure I wanted to know.

"Come see for yourself."

I followed him down the hall, sticking close just in case something pounced. He pushed open a door and I was besieged by a bevy of screeches and squeals, and a pungent, musky smell. White cabinets lined the walls, and at least two dozen glass or wire cages were situated all around the room on top of the cabinets. I identified one dog, two cats, a few birds, some hamsters and—

"Oh my God—are those *rats?*" I stepped behind him and pointed.

Sam followed my finger, then gave me a little smile. "Yeah. This can't be the first time you've seen a rat."

"No, we have those in the city, but we don't make pets out of them."

Sam laughed and jerked his thumb to the right. "I keep the mice and rats around to feed the snakes."

I froze. I couldn't look, I just couldn't look.

His head turned toward the entrance. "That must be the Randalls. Ready?"

"You bet," I said, eager to leave the rodent room. My skin was still crawling when I stopped in the office to pick up my camera. A full-body shiver overtook me, then I trotted behind Sam down the hall. En route, we decided to put Angel in an exam room with food and water to keep her out from underfoot.

The Randalls were an adorable family—mom, dad and two kids, with one on the way. They were distraught over their pet Mister, a cute little beagle whose pain-filled eyes peeked out from under a blanket. Dad Randall and Sam moved Mister from the family's SUV onto a mini-gurney and wheeled the little guy into the clinic. I maintained a respectful distance and clicked a few photos in the low light of dusk.

Dr. Samuel Long had built an impressive facility at the top of his mountain. Despite the disaster in his office, and the questionable choice of animals he kept on-site, the lobby and two exam rooms were squeaky clean and reeking of antiseptic. On an empty stomach, the fumes made me a bit queasy, but I forged on, following Sam, Dad Randall and Mister into an exam room. I was riveted on Sam in his take-charge mode, and was glad to have the excuse of the camera lens to keep looking at him. Between the odor and his aura, I was getting downright light-headed.

"Let's take a look at you, Mister," he said, then pulled back the blanket.

I saw blood, then I saw black.

"HAVE YOU two had sex yet?"

I stared at the phone, then jammed my mouth to the receiver. "Jacki, have you heard a word I've said?"

"He has a girlfriend, he lives on the set of "Bonanza," he maintains a menagerie, and he's saving a family pet as we speak."

"I've been here all of two hours—when do you think we would have had the opportunity or the inclination to have sex?" I wedged the receiver between my ear and my shoulder so I could transfer a piece of unidentifiable chicken to a paper plate while holding an ice bag to my head. "I forgot to mention that I'm also wounded."

"What?"

"I took a dive on the clinic floor at the first sight of dog blood."

"Are you okay?"

"I bumped my head. Sam said I don't have a concussion, but if I start babbling, hang up and call for an ambulance."

"Oooh, did Dr. Long and Strong sweep you up and carry you to safety?"

"No, but he rolled me over and slapped a Band-Aid on my forehead. Then he relegated me to the house to keep me out of the way."

"Oh. Well, where are you staying?"

I licked a dab of mashed potatoes from my finger—hmm, not bad. "There's an apartment over his clinic—Angel and I are staying there with the menagerie. But right now I'm in Sam's kitchen."

At the sound of her name, Angel yipped from beneath the kitchen table where she had barricaded herself against her foreign surroundings and the exuberant barking of Sam's dogs locked a few rooms away. I knew how she felt, and had developed a darting eye in the event the doc kept any no-legged pets at home.

"What's his house like?" Jacki asked.

I scanned the log walls and butcher-block kitchen countertop where I stood doling out "fixin's." "His house is...woody." I looked up. "He has a chandelier made out of something that looks like animal bones—I think maybe it's antlers. And his furniture still has bark on it."

"Sounds cozy. Does it look like his girlfriend lives there?"

"I don't see her underwear in the kitchen, if that's what you mean."

"Have you seen his bedroom?"

"No!"

"Liar."

I sighed. "Okay, I peeked—but only because I was looking for the bathroom."

"And?"

"And the bedroom doesn't have curtains."

"That's a good sign. Did you see girl stuff in the bathroom?"

"I didn't look."

"Liar."

"Okay, I peeked—but only because I was looking for painkiller for my head."

"And?"

"And I didn't see any girl stuff, but there's a bathroom off the master bedroom where his dogs are locked up, so her things could be there."

"Do you think they're serious?"

"I haven't met them, but their barks sound pretty serious."

"Hardee har. I meant the girlfriend."

"It's none of my business," I said primly.

"Right." Jacki didn't bother to hide her sarcasm. "How's the man allergy?"

"Intact." I sniffled for proof. "How was the Jersey shore?"

"Wonderful," Jacki breathed. "I'm so happy, Kenzie. I think Ted is the one."

I worked my mouth from side to side. "That's great, Jacki, really. But does there have to be only one? Can't he be one of the ones?"

"One of the ones?"

"One of the many ones that could be a lifetime partner."

"But I only want *one* lifetime partner."

I rubbed my itching nose, then heard footsteps on the porch outside the kitchen door. "There's Sam now. I'll call you soon."

Jacki was still talking when I hung up the phone. I caught the word *hypochondriac*—or maybe it was *nymphomaniac*—before I slammed down the receiver.

Much foot pounding sounded outside, and I assumed Sam was stomping something rural off his boots. He walked in the door in his sock feet, still wearing the fabulous lab coat over his jeans. He looked tired, but he grinned. "Smells good in here."

I was seized by the bizarre sensation of being a pioneer woman greeting her mountain-man husband at the end of a long day, and had to resist walking over to loop my arms around his neck. It was the painkillers kicking in. "How's Mister?" I asked.

"He's going to be fine." Sam put his warm hand over my hand that held the ice bag on my head and lifted. "The question is, how are you?"

"Just a bump," I said, but my heart was beating double-time at his nearness. "Sorry about passing out on you like that."

He gave me a little smile, but his eyes were dark with

concern as he skimmed his fingers over my bump. "Have you been feeling light-headed?"

"No." At least not until he'd touched me.

"Are you sleepy?"

"More tired than sleepy, I think."

He seemed satisfied that my noggin hadn't been permanently compromised, then he swept my damp hair back from my temple with his thumb. "You've had a long day."

I wet my lips. "So have you."

He wet his lips. "I didn't get to give you a proper welcome."

My mouth opened involuntarily and softened in preparation for his kiss. He landed with authority, awakening every nerve ending in my body. He slipped his arm around my back and pulled me closer as the kiss intensified. My breasts grew heavy and my stomach tingled where his growing erection pressed insistently. When he slid his hand down over the curve of my hip, my throat began to itch, and I remembered all the reasons I couldn't let down my guard...any more than I had.

I dragged myself out of his arms and touched my mouth. "We can't," I said, gasping for breath.

He looked perplexed and his breathing was uneven. "Why not?"

"Because..." I flailed an arm, buying time. "Because I'm here to work, Sam. Fooling around when we didn't know each other was one thing, but now...I can't." I was here for a byline, not a fling.

He pushed his hand into his hair and exhaled noisily. "Okay. We're both adults—we should be able to get through this week without doing something that you'll regret." He grasped the edge of the counter and seemed to grapple for control. I have to admit it gave me a twinge of feminine satisfaction. He inhaled and exhaled a couple of times, then emitted a little laugh. "But if you change your mind, just yell."

A shiver passed through my body as it remembered every wonderful thing he'd done to it that night in the hotel room. I opened my mouth to yell, then clamped it shut and turned back to the chicken. Getting through this week without getting naked with Sam was going to be more of a challenge than I thought.

"Meanwhile," he said, "why don't we sit and eat?" He shrugged out of the lab coat and folded it over the back of his chair. "Would you like tea?" He pulled a plastic gallon jug of it out of the refrigerator, and I nodded. I didn't need the caffeine, but I didn't see any bottled water handy, and I wasn't going to risk the tap—God only knew the source.

Sam's dogs must have heard his voice because their barking increased to a crescendo.

"Settle down in there," he yelled, and they stopped mid-yelp.

I wanted to go home, but instead I asked, "How many dogs do you have?"

"Just three."

"*Just* three?"

He grinned. "Every stray dog in the county seems to find its way here. Between you and me, I think people drop them off at the bottom of the ridge, hoping they'll find their way up here and I'll take them in."

"Do you?"

"Usually. But I try to find homes for them. These three, though, were uglier than most and nobody wanted them, so I decided to keep them. How about some music?"

He didn't wait for my answer, but flipped on a radio on top of the refrigerator. The station was local and folksy, and the music made the space seem more intimate. I was still jumpy from the kiss when I took a seat at the rough-hewn table, a plate of fried chicken, mashed potatoes, green beans and biscuits in front of me. Angel came out from under the table, whining, to lean against my leg.

"She's a little spooked at being in a new place," I said.

He picked up a large piece of chicken with both hands. "I imagine that coming here has been culture shock for both of you, hasn't it?" The grin was back, which eased the tension a bit.

I bristled at the notion that I wasn't worldly. "I see this assignment as a great adventure, a chance to discover new things."

"Oh, I suspect you'll see a few things you've never seen before while you're here."

"Good," I said cheerfully, then bit into what I thought was a chicken leg. The first bite I got nothing but the crinkly, crispy batter, but on the second bite I hit meat. My empty stomach was happy. "You have quite a place here. Did you build it yourself?"

He nodded. "I built the clinic first and lived in the apartment while I finished the house."

Log-home living wasn't my bag, but I appreciated the work that had gone into building it. "Wow...that's amazing."

He seemed amused. "Not really. I like to work with my hands."

My cheeks warmed. I remembered those superb calluses, and now I knew how he'd gotten them. Time to change the subject. "Are you excited about your magazine cover hitting the stands tomorrow?"

He shrugged. "No offense, but I haven't thought much about it."

"Your family and friends must be excited."

Another shrug. "My mom, of course, and some of the

people in town." His eyes danced. "Mostly I expect to get razzed for it."

"By the way, I hear you gave me all the credit for talking you into it. Thanks—you made me look good in front of my boss."

"It was the least I could do after accusing you of setting me up."

I thought about it, then nodded. "You're right."

He laughed and drank from his iced tea glass. "You have to admit that was some coincidence."

I nodded again.

"I assume your boss still doesn't know how we first met?"

"No."

"Well, don't get me wrong—I'm glad you're here, but I was surprised when Ms. Birch called me about your writing an article about me."

I squirmed. "Why would you be surprised that readers would be interested in what you do?"

"I was surprised that you were doing the story. I thought you were her executive assistant."

More squirming. "I am, but I had mentioned to Helena that I wanted to put my journalism degree to use. She thought I was a good fit for the assignment."

"I would say you are a perfect fit," he murmured with a half smile, then shook his head. "Man, this is going to be one long week."

My neck began to itch violently. I scratched like a wild animal, stretching the neck of my sweater to reach as much skin as possible.

"Are you all right?"

"Allergies," I mumbled. "They seem to have gotten worse since I arrived."

"It must be all the pollen. The entire outdoors is having sex right now."

I stopped scratching and began ovulating. "I really should get my antihistamine."

He nodded toward my glass. "Drink up—it's green tea, a natural antihistamine. Three or four glasses of that a day and eventually you can give up your over-the-counter drugs."

I sipped the sweet amber liquid in my glass. "I, um, have this theory about allergies."

"Oh?"

"I think that nature gives us allergic reactions to things that are bad for us."

"An interesting theory," he said. "But many people have reactions to natural substances, such as pollen. And pollen is *not* only not bad for the ecology, it's necessary." He forked in a mouthful of potatoes and swallowed. "If a person is allergic to something natural, his or her chemical makeup is simply flawed—that person's body isn't properly equipped to accommodate the allergen."

My body wasn't equipped to accommodate men? I felt a sneeze coming on and yanked up my napkin just in time to catch a noisy one. The dogs must have taken it as a cue to resume barking, and began howling louder than before.

He laughed. "I guess it's a good thing you'll be here for only a week."

I closed my eyes briefly. My thoughts exactly.

11

"ARE YOU SURE you'll be okay sleeping out here?" Sam asked.

We stood in the apartment over the clinic, and I was gnawing my manicure. The combination sitting room/kitchen, the bedroom and the bathroom were decorated in the same style as the cabin—Early American Timber. But the space was larger than my own place in the city, and featured a washer and dryer, a real treat. At home I lugged my laundry down nine flights of stairs to a row of relic washers in a dank basement. If I'd known about the appliances, I would've brought all my dirty clothes with me.

"It's nice," I said, my gaze darting toward the door. "Thank you for offering me a place to stay."

He put his hands on his lean hips. "Well, there's not much in the form of boarding houses in town, and I thought this would be best since we're going to be spending so much time together. I stocked the refrigerator with food I thought you might like, bagels and cream cheese, bottled water, salad stuff."

"Thank you."

He grinned. "Listen, if having the animals downstairs bothers you, you can stay in the house with me—"

"I'll be fine," I cut in, then bit into my lower lip. "Are you sure they can't get out?"

"Positive."

The man was so sexy, I couldn't breathe. (Plus my nose

was stopped up.) The thought of us undressing and going to separate beds seemed a bit ludicrous considering we already had carnal knowledge of each other, but I kept reminding myself that things were different now. The stakes were higher—my job, my integrity, and maybe, just maybe, my heart.

"What's the schedule tomorrow?" I asked.

"I'm expected at the Brenigar farm at six to treat their herd for pink eye, so we'll need to leave around five-thirty."

"In the morning?" I squeaked. "On Sunday?"

He laughed. "Ed Brenigar has a full-time job during the week, and he farms in between. You don't have to come along if you'd rather sleep in."

"No, I'll be ready," I said, trying to calculate how early I'd have to get up to do my hair, makeup and clothes. I might as well start now.

"Did you bring boots?" he asked.

I nodded, proud.

"You might want to wear them tomorrow."

At least some of my outfit was decided. "Will it take all day?"

"No, just a couple of hours. I thought I'd tackle the mess in my office in the afternoon."

"Will you have time to answer questions for the article?"

"Sure." He pointed. "There's a phone on the nightstand. Feel free to make calls if you need to."

"Do you have a line for business and one for personal use?"

"Naw, people around here would just call my home number anyway. Here's the number to my cell phone." He handed me a slip of paper. "Call me if you get scared."

I laughed. "Scared? Sam, I live in Manhattan. I won't get *scared.*"

He held up his hands. "My mistake. I'll see you in the morning."

He turned to go and panic seized me. "Sam?"

He turned back, his eyes alight. "Yeah?"

"I...um...are there mountain lions around here?"

His laughter filled the room. "Don't worry, Kenzie—I'm the most dangerous animal on this ridge."

On that thigh-twinging note, I said good-night and listened as he tromped down the stairs and locked me up tight with the snakes. I rolled up towels and covered the quarter-inch crack beneath the door. Then I went to the window that was trimmed out with baby logs and, by the dim illumination of the light on the telephone pole, watched Sam walk to the house. Even the athletic way he carried himself was appealing—shoulders back, stride long, step sure. He went in the side door of the house through the kitchen, and I noted he left the porch light on—for me? Longing welled up in my chest, and I wondered why this man so affected me. He wasn't the first good-looking man I'd slept with, and he surely was the least compatible in terms of lifestyle.

Knowing how much I had to lose, why did I still have this unexplainable urge to wrap my legs around his head?

I sneezed into my hanky. Because I was a glutton for punishment. Punishment brought to mind how early I would have to get up, so I flipped off the light and dragged myself to the bed for which four huge trees had given their lives. Angel was zonked out on the floor next to the bed.

Thirty minutes later, I was still wide-awake even though my body ached with fatigue. Christ, it was so *dark.* Twice I turned on the lamp to prove to myself I hadn't gone blind. And the noise—there *was* none. No raised voices or television from the apartment next door, no sirens or shouting from the street, no creaking vents or rattling windows. I suspected the creatures downstairs were doing their thing, but as Sam had promised, I couldn't hear them.

Then I heard a thump and my heart vaulted to my throat. My hand darted out for the phone on the night-stand before I realized the source of the thump. I turned on the light and Angel blinked at me, standing with her front legs against the mattress, thumping her tail on the floor. She whined and I sighed. "Okay, you can sleep with me, but if you start snoring, you're history."

I hauled her into bed with me and she snuggled against my butt. I smiled to myself at the picture of her—or anything—being snuggled against Helena's butt, although I had to admit my boss was a chain of contradictions. On the one hand, she was the hard-nosed, ball-breaking executive, but on the other hand, she consulted a psychic and believed in curses. I had the feeling that sending me to Jar Hollow to man-sit Sam was her way of using my knack for practicality to fix one more thing—to dispel the notion of the curse in her mind. I was a superhero. Da da DA—Pragmatic Girl.

I decided to leave the lamp on, then proceeded to stare at the clock until 2:00 a.m., thinking about the quandary I'd put myself in. At thirty-one, my life was more directionless than at twenty-one. I was starting to wonder if I was a self-saboteur.

The next thing I knew, the Liberty Bell was clanging two inches away from my ear. I sat straight up and Angel launched herself from the bed, cowering in the corner until I shut off the loudest alarm clock ever invented. When my hearing returned, I climbed out of the bed and padded to the window, curious to see what 4:45 a.m. looked like.

Nature was still snoozing. The trees were heavy and silent. The car and the truck glistened with dew. I might have been the only person in the world. Except I could see Sam moving around in the kitchen at the house. The man was an early—and energetic—riser.

Which, I remembered, was why I'd been late to work the morning after our one-night stand.

I pushed thoughts of his lovemaking from my mind as I showered and dressed. The lump on my forehead had shrunk, but had turned an unflattering shade of green that called for thick bangs. Since we were going to visit a farm, I opted for the dressed-down equestrian look. In addition to my red leather boots, I pulled on a knee-length plaid Polo skirt, a gray silk sweater and a red jacket. I pulled my hair back into a neat twist and confined my jewelry to post earrings and a long gold chain with a simple pendant. Nice, understated, unpretentious.

The temperature in the clinic was hospital-cool, so I dressed Angel in a yellow sweater and bow, and took her for a walk around the building by the glow of my combination penlight-alarm-keychain. It was still pitch-black, but based on the strange chirpings and burpings around us, some woodland creatures were beginning to stir. I urged Angel to hurry the hell up, but I didn't have to worry—the ominous surroundings apparently scared the business right out of her. I returned her to the apartment, grabbed my shoulder bag, and met Sam downstairs at 5:30 a.m. on the dot.

He sat behind his piled-up desk, drinking coffee and reading a newspaper that wasn't the *Times*. He looked up. "Good morning. How did you sleep?"

"Fine," I lied. "It's really quiet here."

"Yeah, isn't it great? How's your head?"

"Okay."

"Good." He must have suddenly realized that I was

wearing clothes because he looked me up and down. "That's what you're wearing?"

I balked. "You said to wear boots."

He glanced down at my Stuart Weitzman specials and pushed his tongue into his cheek. "So I did. Want some coffee?"

"Is there a Starbucks along the way?"

"Uh, no."

"Then yes, please."

He stood and poured a John Deere tractor travel mug full of brew. He wore a navy blue Gap T-shirt (I knew T-shirts), and faded Wrangler jeans that were distressed in all the right places. Slap a designer label on those denims and the view would have rivaled any billboard hanging in Times Square.

"I'm out of cream, but I have sugar."

I didn't want to seem high-maintenance, so I shook my head and reached for the mug.

"Let's go, partner," he said, then shrugged into a heavy denim jacket and picked up a big black leather case.

Partner—hmm. Gravel crunched under our footsteps as we walked toward the double-cab truck in the pre-dawn. I was a bit unsteady in my high-heeled boots, but I managed. When we got to the truck, he swung his big bag into the back. A large metal chest sat next to the cab. "Is that where you keep supplies?"

He nodded. "Plus tools and various straps and wrenches, in case an animal has to be subdued."

I hadn't realized his job could be so physical. "Have you ever been hurt?"

"Nothing serious," he said. "A few kicks and a couple of bites." He flashed a grin and opened the passenger-side door for me. "But those were women, not patients."

I smirked and Val Jessum came to mind. The woman had looked as if she could buck.

I focused on trying to figure out how I was going to get up on the seat. Sam took my bag and deposited it first, then directed me to step onto something called a running board and pull myself up with a handy strap hanging down. He still had to help me, and between the unfamiliar movement and his hands on my waist, I was a stiff klutz. I half rolled, half fell onto the seat, but had managed to catch my breath by the time he walked around and swung up into his own seat in one graceful motion.

"Buckle up," he said. "This might be a rough ride."

Later I decided that would be the opening line of my article. "Rough ride" didn't begin to describe the teeth-jarring journey over roads that were little more than mud-caked ditches. I quizzed Sam about his practice, and accidentally bit down on my tongue too many times to count. Twice we had to stop for Sam to take down barbed-wire gates. Admittedly, though, the Brenigar farm offered up some gorgeous scenery, from furrowed fields to enormous sprawling trees to red barns.

"Do the Brenigars raise cows?" I asked.

"Yeah," he said, "but in your article, you might want to use the word *cattle*."

I didn't see the difference, but I made a mental note. We drove past a big white clapboard house and Sam waved at the woman in the yard who was carrying a pail in each hand. He turned onto a dirt path and we lurched over more muddy, rocky terrain. I actually bounced so high on my seat that once I hit my head on the roof of the cab. I saw stars, but I shook it off, reminding myself that I couldn't look after Sam if I sustained a serious head injury.

When we came to a stop in front of another barbed-wire

gate and Sam turned off the engine, even the stillness vibrated.

"I'll come around and help you down," Sam said.

I dug my notebook and camera out of my bag. Sam opened the door and reached for me. My heart raced as he clamped down on my waist. I put one hand on his shoulder and slid down his long, hard body...and kept going. When I looked down, I was ankle-deep in mud that smelled as if it might be spiced with more than just dirt and water.

"Sorry about that," he said.

"It's okay," I murmured, mourning my lovely boots. I lifted one foot with a great sucking noise, only to step forward into more of the same.

Sam retrieved his bag and moved toward the gate, yelling a greeting to someone on the other side. I slipped and slid my way through the muck to catch up with him, and stared at the dozen or so cows—er, cattle—on the other side. They were bigger than the ones I'd seen at the petting zoo.

Ed Brenigar, a thick man with ruddy skin, came to let us through the gate. He shook hands with Sam, whom he called "Doc."

"Ed, this is Kenzie Mansfield. She's writing an article about my practice. Okay with you if she watches?"

"No problem, Doc." The man revealed big, square teeth. "You're turning into a regular celebrity. Hattie's missing church this morning to make sure she's at Chickle's when it opens to get that magazine you're going to be on the front of."

Sam looked sheepish. "Don't give me a hard time, Ed, or I'll raise my fees."

The other man laughed. "Val's going to be riding you hard now, boy."

I watched Sam's reaction beneath lowered lashes, but he ignored the man's gibe as he gestured to the cows. "Are these the only ones in the herd that are symptomatic?"

"Yeah—it's early in the year for pink-eye, so I wanted to get out in front of it."

Sam moved toward one of the cows and I shadowed him warily. I stared at the cows and they stared at me, as if knowing I didn't belong. They reeked of manure, and their black and white coats were peppered with mud. One of them bawled, which set off a group bawl, a frightening sound. The first cow started to back up, but Sam reached out and held it by the mane—I was pretty sure that was the wrong word, but that was all I had.

"Their eyes don't look pink," I said, pulling out my camera.

"This is a mild case," Sam said, then flipped back one of the cow's huge eyelids. "See—it's irritated. It's like conjunctivitis in humans, only...bigger."

I swallowed hard at the sight of the inside-out eyelid, but I managed to snap a picture. Sam removed a huge tube from his bag and proceeded to smear ointment all around the cow's eyes, then moved to the next one. The other cows must have mistaken the medicine for food, because they began to crowd around us. One bumped me from behind, and I freaked out a little. I turned and darted away, and it followed me—at a trot. I shrieked and starting jogging back toward the gate as fast as my boots would allow. Bawling ensued, and I looked back. To my abject horror, all the cows had joined in the chase. I was going to be run down by mad cows—what a humiliating way to go.

"Kenzie, stop running!" Sam yelled behind me. "Stand still!"

Reluctantly, I slowed, then stopped, and closed my eyes. The cows gathered around me, bumping me from all sides with their big warm bodies. My screams were stifled by something constricting my neck. I opened my eyes and watched in dismay as a big cowess took my gold pendant in her mouth. The strength of her swallow yanked my face close to hers as the length of chain disappeared before I could lift it over my head. I saw giant teeth and smelled a hot stench of breath. I was going to be swallowed—what a humiliating way to go.

Suddenly I was yanked backward and Sam had one hand on me, and the other hand down the throat of the cow. When he pulled out his arm, he was holding the pendant, dripping with cow slobber. The cow reeled away, snorting and coughing, and the herd followed her. I looked at Sam and he looked irritated.

I burst into tears. "I'm s-s-sorry."

"It's okay," he said with a sigh, lifting the chain over my head and wiping it with a bandana. "Are you all right?"

I nodded miserably.

"Why don't you wait in the truck while I finish up?"

I nodded more miserably.

Ed Brenigar came running up. "Are you two okay?"

"We're fine," Sam said.

"It was the red jacket," Ed said. "Red makes cattle nervous."

Now they told me.

"Ed, I'm going to walk Miss Mansfield back to the truck—would you mind rounding up the herd again?"

"No problem, Doc—are you okay? You're limping."

He was. "You are," I said.

"Just got stepped on," he said. "It's nothing."

My heart twisted. Great—I was supposed to be watching out for him, and I'd started a stampede and had almost gotten him trampled. I looked at my watch—6:37 a.m. The issue of *Personality* with Sam on the cover had hit the east coast newsstands seven minutes ago.

So far, not so good.

12

"You could have been killed!" Jacki said.

I slumped on the edge of my bed, wearing a robe. A hot shower had not restored my spirit. "I might still die of humiliation."

"How were you to know that red would incite a cow riot? They should teach those things in school! Did your boots survive?"

"Barely," I said, staring at their muddy ruins on a newspaper on the floor. Angel sniffed at them, then turned away whining. "They were last year's style," I said, sighing, "but I loved those boots."

"Of course you did," Jacki crooned. "What's not to love?"

"Sam thinks I'm an idiot."

"He doesn't think you're an idiot. He probably thinks you're...out of your element. Besides, if you don't like this guy, why do you care what he thinks?"

I didn't have an answer for that one.

"Kenzie, are you there?"

"Yes, I'm here." I heard Sam come into the clinic downstairs. "But I have to go—Sam's back with his issue of the magazine."

"I already got my copy," Jacki said. "It's *hot*—women all over the country will be clamoring for this guy."

I frowned. "Bye, Jacki."

I checked the mirror and decided my long terrycloth

robe was discreet enough to greet Sam—he'd certainly seen me in less. I slipped my feet into rhinestone flip-flops and took the stairs two at a time. I had to admit I was eager to see the cover. Angel trotted after me, her toenails clicking on the floor. "How does the cover look?" I called. I rounded the corner and stopped short at the sight of Val Jessum standing in the clinic lobby, holding several issues of *Personality* magazine.

"Oh," I said, feeling a flush climb my cheeks. "I thought you were—"

"Sam?" she asked, her eyes full of suspicion. Her hair was long and curly and wild. She wore a denim mini-skirt, a snug sweater and high heels—I assumed she had not just come from church. Val was scrutinizing my bathroom attire with equal interest—it was probably apparent that I, too, had not been to church this morning.

I clutched my lapels closed. "This isn't what you think."

"What do I think?"

I swallowed. "I don't know—what *do* you think?"

She bit into her cherry-red lip and cocked one hip. Then she lifted her chin and held out one of the magazines. "I think the cover looks great. Arma saved these copies for Sam. She asked me to drop them by."

I hesitated, then took the olive branch she offered and agreed wholeheartedly that the cover looked great. *Hometown Hero!* heralded the full-color glossy photo of Dr. Samuel Long, volunteer firefighter. With his all-American good looks and striking yellow jacket, Sam Long would indeed be stoking fires, not quenching them, from sea to shining sea. I allowed myself a secret thrill that I had experienced the man's proficiency first-hand. With a start I also realized that some of my suggestions for the cover had been implemented, which pleased me even more. "It'll be a bestseller," I cried in my exuberance.

When I looked up, though, instead of pride, I saw fear in Val's eyes. Fear that she was losing Sam to fame? Or maybe to me?

Her throat constricted and her eyes grew moist. "Sam's the best thing that ever happened to this town. I don't know what we'd do without him."

My heart went out to her, and I spoke carefully. "He seems just as fond of Jar Hollow."

She pursed her bee-stung lips. "What's it like, living in the city?"

I almost smiled because "the city" was less than a day's drive away, but I realized that to a woman who had likely lived her entire life in this small town, Manhattan might as well have been on another continent. "It's...hectic."

"Exciting?"

"Yes, and busy. Lots of people and lots of concrete." I hesitated, but felt compelled to put this woman at ease. "I have a confession to make—I had never walked on dirt until I arrived here yesterday."

She guffawed. "You're kidding."

"No, I'm not."

She laughed, and I felt the tension ease a bit. "I've always wanted to go to Manhattan."

"Why haven't you?"

She shrugged. "Family obligations, and after that I guess I was afraid." She wet her lips. "And then Sam came to town."

And after Sam had come to town, she hadn't wanted to leave. And I was her worst nightmare—a city girl invading her territory, distracting her man.

Angel scampered into view.

"Cute dog," Val said, bending over to scratch the pooch's head.

The dog was thrilled to have someone's full attention

and practically moaned in appreciation of the woman's ministrations. A guilty pang struck me. "That's Angel, she belongs to my boss. I brought her to Sam to be spayed—it's one of the reasons I'm here."

Val adjusted the dog's yellow bow. "What are the other reasons you're here?" she asked quietly.

I swallowed. "I'm here to write an article for the magazine about Sam's veterinarian practice."

"That's what Sam said." She gave Angel a final pat and looked up at me. "Is there another reason?"

My mind and heart raced for a response. I certainly couldn't tell her about the cover curse. And I didn't know what my feelings for Sam were or how deep they might run, but neither did I want to lie. "I can honestly say that if my boss hadn't given me this assignment, I wouldn't be here."

"Sam didn't ask you to come?"

"No, he didn't. He agreed to be on the cover of *Personality,* and he agreed to this article only because it will bring publicity to your town."

The sound of Sam's truck pulling in stopped our conversation cold. Val gave me a panicked look, as if she was afraid I would tell Sam about our tête-à-tête. I tried to reassure her with a smile. When he opened the door and walked in, I could tell he didn't know what to expect.

After an awkward couple of seconds, I said, "It's the man of the hour," and held up the issue in my hand. "Val was nice enough to bring you a few copies for your scrapbook."

"Arma told me," he said to Val. "I must have passed you on the road."

"I passed you at Biggs Run and tried to flag you down," she said. "But you were preoccupied."

For whatever reason, they both looked at me, and I felt

ridiculous standing there in my robe. I pointed over my shoulder. "I'm going to get dressed. Goodbye, Val." I fled upstairs, but before I reached the apartment, I could hear their raised voices. Angel's chew toy in the doorway slowed me down long enough to hear Val say, "Who is she to you, Sam?"

I kicked the chew toy aside, then closed the door behind me. I felt extraneous and I inwardly railed against Helena for sending me here and putting me in such an awkward situation. Two seconds later I owned up to the fact that I could have said no to her request. I'd had my own reasons for wanting to see Sam again, I just hadn't expected things to become quite so complicated.

I lusted after the man, plain and simple. Every time I looked at him, I lost my train of thought, and my ability to reason. Untying my robe, I gritted my teeth as even the terrycloth fabric sliding over my skin seemed unbearably erotic. I hated that the man made me want to touch myself, but there it was. I stepped out of my robe and opened my half-unpacked suitcase to find something to wear. While rummaging, my hand closed around the homemade dildo I'd stuffed down in a clean sock. I unsheathed the dildo and sighed at its perfect peachy likeness to the real thing.

Then my own peach got all warm and achy.

I glanced at the locked door, then back to the dildo and concluded in that crazy way a horny person thinks that the reason I was so reactive to Sam was because I needed to release some pent-up sexual frustration. I owed it to myself to use the dildo once before I gave it back.

"Hel-*lo*, Buddy," I murmured, then lay down on the tree-trunk bed. If I couldn't have Sam, then this was surely the next best thing.

I ran my hands over my body pretending it was Sam touching me. When I held the dildo between my thighs, I was shocked at how real it felt. I closed my eyes. It wasn't much of a stretch to picture Sam levering himself over me and pushing his arousal against me, trying to breach my peach and take us both to heaven. I moaned his name and slid his silicone image against my most delicate parts, slick with need from thinking about Sam. I longed for the weight of his body on mine, for his deep, intense kisses, and his voice in my ear, urging me to higher heights.

When the mattress dipped, I was so immersed in my fantasy, I was confused for a split second. Then Sam—flesh and blood—slid on top of me, naked and hard, and whispered, "How about the real thing?"

Somewhere down deep I was mortified that he'd found me this way, but frankly, I was too aroused to be embarrassed. I was already on the verge of climaxing and the knowledge that it was Sam between my thighs practically sent me over the edge. I dropped the dildo on the bed somewhere. He kissed me hard and thoroughly, rubbing his hair-covered chest against my bare nipples until I twisted beneath him. "Now," I murmured. "Now, Sam."

He pulled up my knees to straddle his waist, and with one thrust, filled me completely. We fell into a rhythmic glide that became increasingly frantic. I could feel my climax building, building. He caught my mouth for a plunging kiss, then whispered, "You're killing me—I can't hold out much longer."

I normally give my partner the courtesy of letting him know I'm going to come, but this one hit me so fast, I didn't have time. Still, I trusted that Sam knew what was happening when I screamed his name and the deity at the top of my lungs, then contracted like a spring. His own release seemed just as powerful, at least from the receiver's point of view. He moaned my name and a few unintelligible sounds that were very convincing.

We recovered slowly, muscles twitching, lungs heaving for replenishing oxygen. With eyes closed, I stroked Sam's hair and focused on his breathing near my ear. I bit down on my cheek and willed my heart to ignore this mind-blowing experience. I didn't want it to do something stupid like fall for Dr. Samuel Long, Eagle Scout, Hometown Hero, and cover model extraordinaire. That would sort of wreck my life plans.

I decided if I broke the spell first, I wouldn't appear needy, so I shifted beneath him and he complied, rolling to my side. Still, his hand remained on my stomach.

"The door was locked," I said.

He grinned lazily. "I had a key."

"That's an invasion of privacy."

"Does that carry the same penalty as shirt-stealing?"

I gave him a light punch. "What were you doing lurking outside my door?"

He exhaled loudly and settled deeper into the mattress. "After Val left, I came up to apologize and heard you making noise." His grin widened. "When I heard you say my name, I took that as an invitation." He pushed his nose into my hair and inhaled. "You smell a lot better than when I left this morning."

I winced. "I'm so sorry about the episode at the Brenigars, and especially that you were hurt."

"It's my fault—I shouldn't have taken you with me."

"How am I going to write an article about your practice if I don't go with you?"

He made a noise in his throat. "I'm just glad you're okay."

"Thanks to you."

"Well, now, little lady," he said in a deep, gruff voice, "I *am* a hometown hero."

I laughed. "How's your foot?"

"Fine as frog hair."

I laughed again, then reached under my hip where the dildo had wound up. I held it up. "What do you think?"

He scratched his head and laughed. "I'm more interested in what *you* think."

I saw my chance to tease him. "Well...it'll do in a pinch."

He rolled over and caught my chin with his hand. "Has it been getting a lot of use?"

I swallowed. "Actually, I started feeling bad about the circumstances of its...creation, and I was bringing it back to you. Unused...well, until...recently."

"Bringing it back? What on earth would *I* do with it?"

I shrugged. "I thought maybe you would dispose of it...or give it to...someone close to you." I hesitated, then added, "Like Val."

He frowned. "Okay, first of all, I'd have a hell of a hard time explaining how and why I had something like that in my possession."

I giggled.

"And second, I wouldn't give it to Val. I'm sorry she came by and I hope she didn't say anything to upset you."

I let a few seconds pass before asking, "Are you two an item?"

He made a rueful noise. "Val has always wanted us to be a couple—I don't."

"But you dated?" I felt like a shrew for asking, but reasoned that it was a detail I needed for the article—readers would want to know. I was a reader, and *I* wanted to know.

"Val came to work for me about a year ago as an office manager. She wanted us to become involved, but I didn't think it was a good idea to work and sleep together."

I waited, and he must have seen the "and?" in my eyes.

"And so a couple of months ago, she quit, thinking that if we weren't working together..."

"You could sleep together."

He nodded.

I waited while another unsaid "and?" hung in the air.

"And," he said, "as it turned out, we worked together better than we...er—"

"I get the picture." And *ouch.* I'd assumed they'd slept together, so why had that hurt so much? I sat up and climbed off the bed. "Listen, I don't want to get in the middle of unfinished business."

"You're not." He sat up and reached for me, but I set the dildo on a stump that doubled as a table and shrugged into my robe—there was something creepy about talking about another woman while we were both naked.

"Kenzie, Val is a great girl, but like most small-town girls, she's looking for a commitment. Marriage. Kids. I ended things before they got started because I knew I couldn't give her what she wanted."

No shirt, no shoes, no commitment.

I was so sorry I'd brought it up. An itch on my chest caught my attention and I opened my robe to reveal big pink polka dots. Aside from my nipples.

Sam whistled and came over for a peek. "Looks like hives."

"They are," I muttered. "I'm allergic."

"To what?"

"To, um, you."

He laughed. "What?"

"I had hives all over the first time we...er, you know."

He stopped laughing. "You got hives after we had sex?"

"It doesn't have to be sex. This is what happens when I'm around a...macho man."

"Macho?"

"The more testosterone, the more I react."

He swiped his hand down his face. "This is a new one on me." He stopped. "Wait—does this have anything to do with your 'theory' about allergies protecting you from bad things?"

I shrugged.

He gave a half laugh. "So you think I'm bad for you?"

I closed my robe. "It's nothing personal."

"I disagree." He leaned forward and squinted. "You really believe in this theory of yours, don't you? What—do you think these allergies are some kind of moral check?"

I couldn't correct him to say I thought the allergies were more of an emotional check—to keep me from becoming attached to a man who was commitment-phobic.

"Look," he continued. "If you're afraid that I think less of you because of what happened in New York—"

"I don't," I cut in defensively. "And why should you? I didn't exactly twist your arm."

He held up his hands. "I know, that's not what I meant."

"Then what did you mean?"

He sighed. "I'm making a mess of this. All I'm saying is that we're consenting adults who practiced safe sex. Your skin allergies aren't some kind of punishment for having a good time."

He thought I was an idiot. An easy idiot. I crossed my arms. "Well, in this case, my allergies are a good reminder that I'm here on business, not to play house for a week."

He stood. "Don't be cagey, Kenzie. If you don't want anything like this to happen again, just say so."

"Under the circumstances, I think that would be best," I said primly. I had to keep my long-term goals in mind.

His expression was unreadable, but he nodded curtly. My chest tightened with warring emotions, but I knew it was for the best.

The phone rang, cutting into the tension. Sam let it ring again before snatching it up. "Hello?" He looked up at me, and his expression eased. "Yes, we saw it...yes, it's nice...well, I don't know about that...just a moment." He held the phone out to me. "It's your boss."

I closed my eyes briefly, then walked over to take the receiver. "Hello, Helena."

"We're sold out, Kenzie—the issue *sold out!*"

"Wow, that's great."

"This is what I've been waiting for, Kenzie. This kind of push should give us a couple more percentages of market share."

"Wonderful."

"We can't afford to be distracted now with a cover curse. How is Dr. Long?"

I looked at Sam, but decided "naked and spent" weren't the adjectives that Helena was looking for. He was gathering his clothes, showing signs of a pronounced limp. The bruise on his cow-stomped foot looked ugly and painful. I winced. "He's fine." No thanks to me.

"Taking good care of him?"

He stopped to massage the skin over his breastbone. Panic blipped—his heart. I'd forgotten he had a heart problem and now he was having a heart attack. I had sexed him to death.

He stopped rubbing his chest and stepped into his boxers and jeans. I sighed in relief. No. More. Sex. With. Sam. "Yes, Helena, I'm on top of him—er, *it.*"

Sam gestured he was going to the house and I nodded absently.

"I knew you were the right person for the job, Kenzie."

He walked across the landing and pulled his T-shirt over his head. I saw the chew toy on the top step. He didn't. I dropped the phone. *"Sam, look out!"*

13

"TELL ME he isn't dead," Helena said an hour later when I had called her back, as promised.

I massaged the bridge of my nose and leaned against Sam's desk. "No, Helena, Sam isn't dead, or hurt, thank goodness. Just bruised." The man would be black and blue by the time I went home.

"Kenzie, you're supposed to be watching him!"

"I can't be with him every second of the day!"

"Is he going to be able to perform Angel's surgery tomorrow?"

"It's still on his schedule, Helena."

She made a rueful noise. "Has he gotten any calls from the tabloids?"

I looked at his machine—the display said he had seventeen messages waiting. "I don't know."

"Can you find out?"

I sighed. "Maybe—I have to go."

"Will you put Angel on the phone please?"

I frowned. "Angel?"

"Yes, I'd like to speak to her."

I looked down at the dog, who sat holding her brush in her mouth. I was derelict in my duties. "It's for you," I said dryly, then picked her up and set her on the desk. I held the receiver up to her perky little ear.

"Helloooo, Angel," I heard Helena say in a piercing, falsetto voice. "Mama misses you, yes she does, yes she does. Do you miss Mama?"

"Speak," I whispered, on the chance that she'd been trained. Angel barked into the phone.

"Oh, you do?" crooned Helena. "Is Kenzie taking good care of you, darling?"

"Speak," I whispered, and Angel offered up another affirmative.

"That's good, Angel. You're my little wittle Angel, yes you are, yes you are."

The dog yawned and my opinion of her raised a notch. I put the phone back to my mouth. "Helena, say goodbye." I held the phone to the dog's muzzle again.

"Goodbye, Angel."

"Speak," I whispered, and the dog barked twice. "Nice touch," I said, then hung up the phone.

I heard Sam come into the lobby, so I stuck my head out of the office and looked down the hallway to watch him set down two file boxes. I was going to help him get organized. The muscles in his arms and back moved under his T-shirt, and I fought like hell not to get turned on. "Sam, you have lots of voice messages—want me to sort through them?"

"Sure," he said with a shrug. "Just save the ones that sound important."

He left, I assumed, to retrieve more boxes. I felt a little guilty listening to his messages, but if he didn't care...

Beep. "Doc, this is Arma. I'm saving some copies of the magazine for you. Just come by when you can."

That was old, I deleted it.

Beep. "Sam, this is John. Nice magazine cover, bro." John laughed. "I hear through the grapevine that you've got *company* this week. Behave."

I kept that one.

Beep. "Sam, honey, it's me." I recognized Val's voice. "I'd really like to talk to you about...us. Give me a call."

The message predated her visit this morning, but I kept it. That entire situation still had me unnerved, probably because even though Val Jessum and I came from different worlds, we were more alike than different. Sam's comment about her wanting a commitment because she was a small-town girl had hit me. It might be true, but small-town girls didn't have the corner on commitment.

Beep. "Sam, it's Mom."

I perked up, telling myself that mothers in general interested me, and analyzing the voice of Sam's mom didn't imply anything in particular.

"I'm looking at your picture on the magazine and I'm just so proud of you, son." She sighed musically. "I know you're busy with your animals, love, but I hope you're taking care of your own health. Don't let this cover business add too much stress to your life. Call me later in the week. Bye, now."

She sounded perfect—supportive, yet concerned, expressive, but not smothering. And she would most certainly dislike me for miring her son in this cover situation. I kept the message and brushed Angel's long coat while I zipped through the next few messages from local well-wishers. Then it came.

Beep. "Dr. Long, this is Terrence Mayo from the *National Keyhole.*" I stopped brushing—a tabloid reporter. "I'd like to talk to you at your earliest convenience. There could be some money in it for you."

My hand hovered over the delete button, then, telling myself that Sam wouldn't be the kind of man to respond to a tabloid reporter, I hit the button. "Message deleted," said a mechanical voice.

There were three calls regarding four-legged patients

that I kept and a couple of hang-ups—from Val?—that I deleted. The last message was the tabloid reporter again, his voice a little more urgent, and I got rid of that one, too.

"Message deleted."

"Telemarketer?" Sam asked behind me.

I jumped and spun around. Had he heard the message? "Uh-hmm," I murmured. "And I deleted a few hang-ups. The others you should listen to."

"Anything urgent?" he asked, dropping a couple of file boxes on the only available space on the floor. Dust motes spiraled up.

"Not that I could tell," I said, then sneezed three times in succession.

"Bless you," Sam said, then fingered a button on my blouse. "How are those hives?"

I inhaled to steel myself against his sex appeal. "Better now that the medicine has kicked in."

He grinned. "Maybe I should take a look?"

Despite the thrill that ran down my back, I flicked his hand away. "Maybe we should get down to work."

He made a face, then jerked his thumb toward the hallway. "I have another box of supplies to carry in. I'll be right back." As he walked away, his phone rang. He started toward it, and my heart blipped in panic—what if it was the reporter? "I'll get it," I offered. "I'm, uh, expecting Helena to call."

"Sure," he said with a shrug. "If it's for me, just take a message." He kept walking.

I picked up the receiver with wet palms, and took my time answering until Sam's footsteps had faded. "Dr. Long's office."

"Dr. Long, please," said a male voice.

My pulse picked up. "May I ask who's calling?"

"Terrence Mayo."

I swallowed hard. "From the *National Keyhole?*"

"I see you got my messages."

My mind raced. "Why do you want to speak with Dr. Long?"

He chuckled wryly. "Just tell the doc that he might be the victim of a *curse.*"

"Hold on, please." I covered the mouthpiece with my hand and closed my eyes, reminding myself that I was here on assignment. My first priority was the magazine, which meant squelching this curse rumor. I uncovered the mouthpiece. "Dr. Long doesn't believe in such nonsense and respectfully asks that you buzz off."

Silence, then, "Even if there's a chance he's in danger?"

"Don't call here anymore," I said, then slammed down the phone.

"Tiff with the boss lady?" Sam asked, sidling through the door carrying a huge box.

I started guiltily. "I have a love/hate relationship with Helena. Do you need a hand?" I stepped after him, wiping my sweaty hands on my dry-clean-only pants.

"Sure—these are new accessories for the snake aquarium."

I stopped dead in my tracks. "On second thought, I'll get started in here."

His laugh was muffled as he made his way down the hall toward the menagerie. I turned and leaned against the doorway, surveying the disaster he called a workspace. How he got anything done in here, I didn't know. I shook my head, but I was actually looking forward to helping him get organized. *To help assuage your guilt,* my conscience taunted.

My motivation didn't matter, I rationalized. What mattered is that everyone got what they wanted. Helena. Sam. Me.

Me? Was I getting what I wanted?

"Okay, partner, I'm ready," Sam announced, clapping his hands together.

He scanned my outfit—pink and white ruffled Yves St. Laurent blouse, dusty-pink hipsters, and white strappy Prada slides. (I did not adhere to the fashion adage "don't wear white shoes before Memorial Day or after Labor Day.")

"I'm not complaining about the view," he said, "but are you sure you want to work in those clothes?"

I looked down. "What's wrong with these clothes?"

"Just that they're a little fancy for office-cleaning."

"I don't clean," I corrected, wagging my finger. "I supervise."

He laughed, then grimaced and touched his shoulder.

"Are you sore?"

"I probably will be tomorrow."

I sighed. "I'm sorry about leaving Angel's chew toy on the stairs."

He scoffed. "Kenzie, it was an accident. I should have been looking where I was going."

I bit into my lip. Actually, *I* was supposed to be looking where he was going.

He put his hands on his hips and scanned the piled-high office. "Where do we start?"

I looked around. "Where do you keep your computer?"

"Computer?"

I blinked. "You don't have a computer?"

He scratched his head. "I've been meaning to buy one, but never quite got around to it."

"PDA?"

"Pardon me?"

"Personal digital assistant."

"Come again?"

I sighed. "Do you have a beeper?"

"Um...no." He patted a hand radio on his belt. "But all the volunteer firefighters have walkie-talkies."

I looked at his belt, then made a self-indulgent detour across his crotch before lifting my gaze. "How is a walkie-talkie connected to your business?"

"It isn't, but it's cool."

I closed my eyes briefly, and when I opened them, he had adopted a rather sheepish expression.

"The truth is, I have a good practice here, but the paperwork is killing me." He grinned. "I need someone like you to cover me."

I wanted to tell him that at the moment I was spread rather thin with cover duties, but instead I held out my hand. "Give me your credit card."

His eyebrows shot up.

"You need equipment," I said. He complied. I handed him my PDA to play with (the best way to get someone interested in technology, I'd found) and directed him to start organizing his patient files while I went upstairs to my room and booted up my own laptop. Accessing the Internet across a dial-up line was a lesson in patience, but I managed to order a desktop computer, accounting and scheduling software, and one of those multi-function printer/scanner/fax machines for express delivery. Since I was already on the Net, I jumped over to the Neiman Marcus Web site and, with my own credit card, ordered a delicious pair of Ferragamo low-heeled boots for Sam. I reasoned he would have ordered them himself if he'd had a computer.

I returned to the office to find him knee-deep in files, my PDA set off to the side—so maybe technology wasn't irresistible to everyone. I pitched in to help sort the files, and he was appreciative, but I could tell the administrative side of the business put him in a dour mood. An hour later my hands were gritty and gray from handling so much paper, but we had made much progress.

Suddenly his phone rang. My heart ratcheted up a notch, thinking it might be the reporter again, but there was no way I could pick it up without diving across Sam and raising his suspicions.

Sam juggled the receiver to his ear. "Hello?" I held my breath, and watched as his face turned serious. "When?...How far along?" He stood and checked his watch. "Tell Watt I'll be there in twenty minutes."

He hung up the phone. "Watt Hendron's mare is about to foal and she's having trouble."

"I'm right behind you," I said, reaching for my camera and notepad.

He hesitated. "This could get messy."

"If you think I'm spending one more minute alone with the snakes than I have to, you're crazy."

He shrugged. "If you think you can handle it."

My chin went in the air. "I can handle it."

"Okay, partner, let's go."

As I climbed into the truck, I said, "Just to clarify—we're going to see a horse, right?"

I SUSPECTED I might be in trouble when Sam put on a rubber glove that went up to his shoulder, and not for a fashion statement. I'd seen my fair share of PBS specials on animals birthing in the wild, but those PG-rated shows hadn't exactly prepared me for the goo, the slime and the smell of a large animal being brought into the world. This foal was "turned," which meant it wasn't in the right position to be squeezed out naturally. I stared in morbid fascination as Sam stuck his arm into the mare's you-know-what, then felt all around, and none too gently. I had to cross my legs.

As soon as Sam pulled out his arm, the mother-to-be, a giant brown beauty, lay down on her side in the large straw-lined stall. Her tail had been bound up, and her coat glistened with sweat. Sam patted her rump. "It won't be long now, Lily."

He peeled off the soiled glove and washed up in a bucket of warm water. Watt Hendron left to get more water, and Sam motioned me closer.

I swallowed hard. "Are you sure I should be this close?"

"I thought this was supposed to be an adventure."

I stepped up carefully, keeping an eye on Lily, who whinnied occasionally and flinched violently.

"You'll be in a good position to catch all the action," he said.

He was right, I realized, and crouched to get a photo of him with Lily in the background. No sooner had I clicked the shutter than I heard the horse shudder and fluid shot out of her like a cannon, dousing my Prada slides with slimy baby juice. I covered my mouth with my fist to keep from gagging.

"Here it comes," Sam said, and two little horse legs appeared, then a head, then the shoulders, then the whole baby slid out with a rush of fluid. It was covered in white gook and smelled…really bad.

"I'm going to be sick," I murmured, then tried to stand. I slipped on the slime and flailed backward, sitting down in the bucket of wash-up water. At least it was warm, I told myself.

"Are you all right?" Sam called.

I knew he was too busy to deal with me, so I said, "Fine," and thrashed my arms until I created enough momentum to free myself. I was soaked from the butt down and the chilly air instantly turned my cool hipsters into a clammy vacuum, but amazingly, I still had the presence of mind to take a few candid photos of Sam cleaning the foal.

"I've seen this a hundred times," he said, "and it never gets old."

The camera lens gave me enough distance to regain my composure, and what I saw made my heart swell. Sam handled the animal as delicately as a flower, the look of awe on his face inspiring. I didn't have to wonder what kind of father he would make, but I did wonder if he'd ever get that chance considering his attitude on commitment.

I got all warm and spongy inside, stirred by the dichotomy of the man. He was without a doubt the most masculine guy I'd ever known intimately, yet he had all the makings of the sensitive type. I was philosophical when I remembered our lovemaking this morning—was it possible for sex to be that exciting within the context of a committed relationship, or were we socially and biologically conditioned to accept and expect wild sex and commitment to be mutually exclusive?

When the foal wobbled to its feet, Sam came over to stand next to me. His breathing and color were heightened by the exertion. Sweaty and covered with bits of straw, he'd never looked more handsome. He turned to me and grinned, and my breath caught in my chest. *Oh, God, don't let me fall in love with this man.*

"Don't mind me," I said to distract him just in case he could read my mind. "I'm going to finish up this roll of film." I stepped back, out of the stall and into a dirt-packed hallway, and raised my camera for a different angle.

"Be careful, Kenzie," Sam said. "There's a lever—"

My hip hit something metal that gave way with a creaking noise. I heard something move overhead and looked up to see a window-sized piece of wood hurtling toward my head.

My mind said to move, but my feet were frozen. Then a locomotive hit me from the side and I landed with a *whoomph* on the packed ground. Oxygen vacated my compressed lungs, and I saw starbursts. I gasped like a fish on dry land, and sat up with a bad feeling pressing on my heart. Sam had knocked me out of my shoes to save me and for his effort, had been clobbered by the piece of wood that was wrapped with a chain and connected to some kind of pulley mechanism that I'd dislodged.

My heart stalled. I'd killed him for sure this time.

14

"SO WHAT *was* the thing that he saved you from?" Jacki asked over the phone, her voice croaky—I'd shamelessly dragged her from a deep sleep before her alarm had gone off in order to relate the previous day's events.

I sighed and laid my head back on my pillow. From this angle in the pre-dawn light, the tree-trunk four-poster bed looked a little ominous. I decided this was as close to camping as I wanted to get. "It was some kind of oversized dumbwaiter to lower grain from the top of the barn. I inadvertently hit a lever and brought it tumbling down."

"That's so exciting!"

"Jacki, Sam could have been killed!" That one thought had kept me awake all night.

"But he wasn't."

"He could have been!"

She yawned. "Better him than you, friend. I think it was a very heroic thing for him to do."

"Yes, but I'm supposed to keep him *away* from danger, not bring it down on his head! Sam would probably be safer if I just went home." I felt a crying jag coming on.

"Well, maybe you should."

"Maybe I should what?"

"Come home."

I bit into my bottom lip and rode through the uneasy feeling that bloomed in my chest. "I would," I said, toying with the hem of the bed sheet, "but I haven't finished the article yet."

"I thought the article was simply your cover."

"No," I said quickly, "I'm going to use the article as a career stepping stone."

"Ah. When did you sleep with him?"

I blinked. "Huh?"

"Don't be coy—I know something happened."

"That's ridic—"

"Spill it."

"Okay," I conceded. "Something happened, but it was accidental."

"Accidental? Did you two mistake each other for something else in the dark?"

"No."

"What then?"

I squirmed. "It wasn't planned. On Sunday he sort of...walked in on me...and the dildo."

"No, he didn't."

I cringed. "Yes...he did."

I heard a choking sound, then a thud and distant laughter. She'd dropped the phone.

"Jacki," I yelled, "you're not helping!"

I heard a rustling sound, then she was back on the line. "*How* did he happen upon you and the dildo? What—were you playing with yourself in the hallway?"

I rolled my eyes. "No, I was in my bedroom."

"And?"

"And he...came to the door to talk to me and he...heard me."

Jacki squealed. "So he broke down the door and ravished you?"

"No," I said miserably. "He had a key and my full cooperation."

"And was it as good as before?"

"Yes. And he didn't have a heart attack, thank goodness. Although, one could perceive that as an insult."

"You're really sick, you know that?"

I winced. "I know, I'm so confused. Helena sent me here to keep Sam out of trouble and so far all I've done is *cause* trouble. For both of us."

"What happened to the girlfriend?"

"He says they're not a couple, but I don't believe him."

"Why not?"

"She dropped by his house last night to see him."

"You were spying?"

"*No.* I was simply looking out the window."

"Uh-huh. And did she spend the night?"

"How would I know?"

"Because you were spying."

I sighed. "Okay, *no,* she didn't spend the night. I happened to be looking out the window again when she left a few minutes later."

"Uh-huh. So she's still hung up on him. What does it matter?"

"It doesn't."

"So why are you worried?"

"I'm not worried."

"You sound worried."

"Okay, I'm *not* worried about a girlfriend, but I'm worried about...everything else."

"You're worried about falling for this guy?"

I frowned. "No. I'm worried about my job, my career, my future."

"Uh-huh. So what's on the schedule for today—sheep dipping?"

"I don't know. We're supposed to make a couple of house calls this morning, then Angel is scheduled to be fixed this afternoon." From where she snuggled next to my butt, Angel lifted her head and whined. I gave her a comforting pat, woman to woman-dog.

"That's a little sad, don't you think?" Jacki asked. "Taking away her ability to have babies?"

"Since when have you been big on babies?" A thought burst into my brain. "You're not—"

"No, I'm not pregnant, Kenzie. But...Ted did ask me last night my thoughts on having a family."

"And what did you say?" I held my breath because among the four of us, Jacki had been voted Least Likely Ever to Own a Breast Pump.

"I told him it sounded appealing."

My mouth opened in surprise. "Wow...that's..." I couldn't pretend. "Confusing, actually. Aren't you the one who said there should be a leash law for children under twelve?"

Jacki sighed musically. "I'm telling you, Kenzie, meeting the right man changes a woman's perspective. Lately I've even been combing the real estate listings for a little house in the burbs."

My eyeballs popped. "The *burbs?* This sounds serious."

"I think it might be."

At the wistfulness in her voice, jealousy twinged through my chest just prior to friendship kicking in. "That's great, Jacki. Really."

She sighed. "I don't mean to be riding you about Sam Long. I'm just so happy with Ted, I guess I'm projecting onto my friends. But you and Sam are such opposites, it would probably never work out."

"Right," I mumbled.

"Maybe the guy in your office who asked you out is Mr. Right—what was his name?"

"Daniel Cruz."

"Yeah. You like him, don't you?"

"I guess so." I hadn't thought of him since I arrived in Jar Hollow.

"You said you weren't allergic to him, so maybe he's the one."

"Maybe." I squinted, but couldn't conjure up his face.

"Let me know if you decide to come home early."

"Thanks for letting me ramble. I think I'm overreacting to everything because I'm homesick."

"Uh-huh. Good luck this morning. Try not to kill yourself. Or anyone else."

I smirked into the phone. "Bye."

I hung up and squeezed my eyes tight against the barrage of emotions hammering in my head. Sam and I hadn't talked much after I'd clobbered him with the hand elevator, although he assured me that other than a headache, he was fine. In fact, when we'd arrived back at his place last night after dark, he'd hinted that he wouldn't mind some company in a hot shower. My raw and reeking body had leapt to attention, but I had resisted his sexy grin. Then his grin had disappeared and he'd asked if I was still stuck on my man allergy theory. I said I was, and he said good night.

I had then barricaded myself in my room against snakes and seducers, stripped my ruined clothing, and soaked in a tub of hot water until the distinctive scent of horses had been poached from my pores. After dutifully checking in with Helena and facilitating another conversation between her and Angel, I'd booted up my laptop to begin outlining the article that was supposed to reorder my career.

An hour later, all I'd been able to come up with was an orderly column of Roman numerals. I was disgusted with myself because I'd dreamed of getting a break like this, and now that I'd been offered the chance to write an article for the magazine, I was coming up empty. My fickle attention had kept straying to the drawer that held the homemade dildo. Instead of giving in to the temptation of "enjoying" the toy, I had walked over to the window to stare at Sam's house. Light flooded the first floor, and through the large windows, I had caught sight of him in jeans, barechested, walking from the kitchen to the living room with a beer in one hand and a magazine in the other hand, his pack of barking dogs moving behind him like...a pack of dogs. (I was going to have to brush up on similes before completing the article.)

I couldn't see what Sam was reading, but I was certain it wasn't the copy of *Personality* magazine that bore his picture. Most likely, it was a medical trade journal of some kind—stacks of them cluttered his office. The man's complete lack of vanity coupled with his noble nighttime reading material made my heart curl up at the pointy end. This man was *real.* I had the sad suspicion that I would spend the rest of my life comparing guys to Dr. Samuel Long.

I'd looked back to my blank computer screen and decided to pay Sam a late-night visit, just to clarify a few details for the article. I'd reasoned it would jumpstart my creativity.

Unfortunately (or, in hindsight, *fortunately*), just as my feet were on the verge of moving, car headlights had appeared. A white sports car had parked on the other side of Sam's truck, and I'd watched with morbid fascination as Val Jessum had unfolded her long sexy self from the interior and made her sway—I mean, *way*—to Sam's door. She'd knocked, then turned to look in the direction of the clinic, straight at me, I'd felt. I'd dived away from the window, then crawled back and peeked over the sill. I'd missed their greeting, but it couldn't have been too contentious since he'd invited her inside.

Sure, she'd left twenty-three minutes later, but that was enough time to...stake her claim. Maybe twice.

Due to Val's visit, I had opted to skip the late-night interview. I'd climbed into bed and donned a sleep mask against the light of the lamp that I'd left on, but I hadn't slept well. For two days I'd been mulling Sam's answer to Val's question *"What is she to you?"* At the time, eavesdropping had seemed rude—and risky. I hadn't wanted to hear him say that I was a one-night stand that wouldn't go away. Then after our...*interlude* Sunday, I had allowed myself to think that maybe his answer had been...something else.

Now I knew it hadn't been, else Val wouldn't have felt welcome to drop by.

With Jacki's advice to come home ringing in my ears, I lugged my pathetic self out of bed, splashed my face with ice-cold water and dressed with care. My yellow wool slacks and my beloved mohair sweater would be comfortable and warm. I donned my most sensible shoes, suede Via Spiga loafers. I had learned my lesson with the jewelry, and chose small understated pieces. I had to use more foundation than usual to cover the circles under my eyes, which led to more mascara, blush, et cetera. To keep my hair out of the way, I rolled it into a French twist and secured it with a dozen little butterfly pins and a half can of hairspray.

I finished early enough to drop two halves of a bagel into the toaster, but while I chewed, Angel started whining and pawing at the door for her morning walk. Strange, since I'd had to take her out last night for an uncharacteristic late pee. I reasoned she was still acclimating to these bizarre surroundings. I pulled the snake-proof stuffing away from the crack under the door and listened for telltale slithering on the other side before opening the bedroom door armed with a stick I'd found outside. Satisfied that nothing had escaped its cage and made its way upstairs, I walked to the lower level and let Angel out to do her thing.

"Good morning."

I gasped and raised my killer stick, then relaxed when I saw it was only Sam walking toward the clinic wearing jeans and a long-sleeved white jersey and carrying an armful of reading material.

"Easy now, I'm not going to get you." Then he grinned. "Unless you want me to."

How could he *do* that? Manage to take me from fear to desire in the space of two seconds? I lowered my highly evolved weapon. "You startled me."

His laugh rode on the morning air. "You should try to relax."

"What's on the schedule this morning?"

"I'm going to the pound to give immunizations. Are you up for it?"

"Sure."

He looked up and down my clothes. "Is that what you're wearing?"

I glanced down at my outfit. "Does yellow also incite stampedes?"

"No," he said with another laugh. "And you look great."

I tingled. "Thanks."

"It's just that..."

"What?"

"Well...do you own a pair of jeans?"

"Of course. Two pairs, in fact."

"Did you bring them with you?"

"No." In truth, I'd spent a fortune on my Seven jeans, and saved them to wear for the most special occasions.

He scratched his head. "Jar Hollow doesn't offer much in terms of shopping, but there are a couple of places where we could pick you up some more casual clothes."

"I'm fine," I said primly.

"Okay." He pointed toward the clinic door. "I'll be in my office when you're ready to go."

I nodded and watched him walk up to the door, wipe his feet on the welcome mat, and disappear inside the clinic. This was his world, I realized with a sad resignation. Trees and animals and solitude. I couldn't help but feel his talents and charm were wasted in this small town and wondered if he ever got bored with his life. It was a patronizing thought, I conceded, but Jar Hollow wasn't exactly the epicenter of anything. I would go crazy living here. Where was the excitement, the stimulation?

The stimulation that Sam could provide notwithstanding.

I walked to the edge of the woods, keeping an eye peeled for Angel's orange sweater. Sam kept the clinic at a sterile temperature, so I bundled her up every day to make sure she was warm.

The spring temperatures had regressed, and a light frost tinged the ground. My nostrils threatened to stick together as I breathed in the morning air—sweet and still. I was surprised to realize that I wasn't nearly as frightened as when I'd first arrived, and in fact, the trees that surrounded Sam's hilltop clearing now seemed...comforting. Granted, things were less intimidating in the early-morning light. Since Angel had ventured out of sight, I decided that even she must be getting braver. "Angel?"

Her answer was a deep growl off to my right. I spotted her orange sweater through the underbrush, then I saw a bush move nearby and the tail of a black cat swish into view. Another stray dropped off to make its way to Sam's clinic, no doubt. I smirked at the thought of Angel squaring off against a cat that was probably equal to her in size. "Angel, come out of there before you get scratched."

But Angel's growl only intensified, then she began barking frantically.

"Angel!" I chastised, taking a tentative step toward the pair, while keeping an eye out for creepy-crawlies on the ground. "Leave the kitty alone, and she'll leave you alone."

But the barking continued, loud and shrill. I wasn't afraid because I was more of a cat person than a dog person, and was confident I could calm the poor feline if she'd let me get close enough. I forged ahead, stepping carefully to protect my pricey loafers.

"Hey," Sam said behind me. "What's all the noise about?"

I turned to see him standing on the porch. "Angel found a stray cat."

"With all that ruckus, you'd think she'd never *seen* a cat."

"Maybe she hasn't," I called over my shoulder, stepping closer. I had the vague sense of Sam hurrying our way. I used my stick to part the bushes. When the cat turned toward me, I realized that it was a strange-looking cat.

In fact, it wasn't a cat at all.

15

"SKUNK!" I yelled stupidly, as if Angel would understand. I stumbled backward and fell on my tailbone. What I had thought was a fluffy cat's tail shook violently, and Angel's barking ended abruptly with a yelp. A wet spray caught me across the lower legs. From behind, Sam yanked me to my feet just as I was overcome with an indescribable odor so intense, my eyes burned and my lungs rebelled.

"Oh, man," Sam said behind me, groaning.

Angel shot past us, and Sam half dragged me away from the skunk's vicinity. We didn't stop until we were at the side door of his log cabin.

"Stay here," he said, gasping for fresh air.

My head was swimming from lack of oxygen. I nodded and gulped air, then tried to calm Angel, who pawed at her nose and rolled in the grass uncontrollably. I was considering joining her when Sam came back dragging a big metal basin behind him, and carrying a can of something.

He dropped the basin on the ground. "Put your clothes in here."

I frowned and lifted my arm. "This is mohair—you can't wash it."

He pursed his mouth and I decided I didn't want to know what was running through his head. "I'm not going to wash it," he said calmly. "I'm going to *burn* it."

My eyes bugged. "Burn it?"

"All of our clothes will have to be burned," he said, pulling his jersey over his head. "There's no saving them."

I was caught between mortification over losing my sweater and distraction over seeing Sam without his shirt. I looked all around and realized he intended for us to disrobe on the spot.

"Don't get modest on me," he said, sitting down to untie his boots. "The sooner you get out of those clothes, the less the smell will seep into your skin and hair."

That got me moving. I pulled off my sweater and reluctantly dropped it in the basin on top of his shirt. He tossed his boots on the pile.

"Shoes too?" I asked with a moan.

He nodded. "I'm afraid so."

Shivering in the cold, I slipped out of my shoes, slacks, and trouser socks, and dumped them with a whimper.

"Her sweater, too," he said, nodding toward Angel, who lay on her stomach with her paws over her eyes. I disrobed her to the tune of whining complaints, trying not to think about how I looked, standing in my underwear in the middle of his yard. The icy cold of the ground seeped up through the soles of my feet. I hopped from foot to foot, which I'm sure made me look even more sexy.

Sam, on the other hand, looked like an underwear model in his snug briefs, pouring thick black liquid all over our clothes. He struck a match and dropped it in, igniting an instant low fire. The mohair sweater that had cost me a week's paycheck caught fire and disintegrated.

"Let's go inside and try to wash this off," Sam said.

He was irritated, I could tell. I didn't blame him—Angel and I had been nothing but trouble since the moment we'd arrived. Maybe Jacki was right—maybe I should just go home, for Sam's sake and for mine. Pondering, I picked up Angel, whose coat reeked, and followed Sam into the house. His motley collection of ugly dogs came running to greet us, but their barks became snorts and sneezes when they got a whiff.

"The tub in my bathroom is bigger," Sam said, pointing. "Run it full of warm soapy water and get in."

I walked into his bedroom and closed the door behind me to keep the dogs out. His room was stocked with clubby, masculine furniture, a colorful handmade quilt on his humongous bed, and a thick green braided rug on the wood floor. A fish with a mouth wide enough to stick my head inside was mounted on a board over his bed. Yikes. But fish or no, I could picture me and Sam in that big slab of a bed, playing hide and seek. The man was an unlimited source of fantasy.

Unfortunately, the thought of him and Val Jessum romping in the bed so recently gave me pause.

I shook myself into action and padded into his bathroom, a sparse but comfortable room featuring a glassed-in shower and a gigantic claw-foot bathtub situated next to a picturesque bay window. I inhaled, hoping to smell Sam's scent, but my olfactory glands apparently had shut down. Angel squirmed in my arms and I set her down while I started the water running. I opened a closet door that was made out of the same raw planks as the walls with the express intention of looking for bubble bath or liquid soap, but I kept my eyes peeled for any indication of a frequent female visitor.

Yes, I was obsessing, but I couldn't help it. And I told myself it really didn't matter since, at this rate, Sam was probably going to send me home before I had a chance to burn down his house.

The closet revealed a stack of white towels and washcloths, plus an arsenal of rubbing alcohol and disinfectant soap, surgical gloves (?), cotton balls, swabs, razors, his familiar sport-scent deodorant and other manly toiletries. Not a tampon or scrunchie in sight. Ditto for the medicine cabinet. I dumped the disinfectant soap in the tub and swirled the water with my hand to whip up some bubbles, then debated on whether to strip my underwear before getting in. The suds looked sufficient to cover me if Sam came in, and frankly, I wanted to start scrubbing off the skunk smell.

I stripped and stepped into the warm water, eased down and dunked my head, then worked a handful of shampoo into a lather. Unfortunately, the warm water seemed to intensify the skunk odor, and no matter how hard I scrubbed, I couldn't seem to stay ahead of it. Angel stood with her front paws on the edge of the tub and cocked her head at me. I glanced at her defiled long silky coat and wondered how many doggie shampoos it would take to make her tolerable. If I returned Angel smelling like a country hound, Helena would kill me and *then* fire me.

A knock sounded, sending my pulse into overdrive. Angel abandoned me and trotted to the door. I arranged the washcloth and the bubbles around me in a futile attempt to cover my girlies, then called, "Come in."

Sam stuck his head inside. "How's it—" he stopped and raked his gaze over me "—going in here?"

I flushed and shifted, sending my protective bubbles to the opposite end of the tub. "I don't think I'm making much headway—the odor is still strong."

His eyes smoldered and he seemed distracted for a few seconds. A shiver shook my shoulders and sent goose bumps over my skin. The air hummed with sexual current, and I was struck with an overwhelming sense of intimacy, being naked in this man's bathtub in a log cabin that he'd built with his own hands on the top of a mountain. We could have been the only two people in the world.

Angel barked.

The only two people in the world, and a dog with a bad sense of timing.

"Can I come in?" he asked. "I brought something to help with the smell."

I nodded, still hugging myself. "Is it some kind of medicine or chemical?"

"Sort of." He pushed open the door, set down a metal basin, and hefted a huge jar of red liquid. "Tomato juice."

I frowned, mostly because the jar was obscuring his abs. "Are we making bloody Marys?"

He laughed. "No. Tomato juice will neutralize the odor." I must have looked skeptical, because he added, "You'll have to take my word for it." He unscrewed the lid, then walked to the tub, hoisting the jar. "You might want to close your eyes."

I did, and tensed. I'd thought having tomato juice poured over my head was going to be unpleasant, but actually...it was worse. Cold, slimy, clumpy, and salty. I clawed the stuff out of my eyes and slouched in abject misery. My friends simply would not believe this.

"Just sit for a few minutes and let the juice work," he said. "I'll see what I can do with Angel."

"She doesn't like baths," I said. "When I took her to the groomer's, she escaped and turned the whole place upside down. She was missing in action for almost a half an hour before we tracked her down."

He looked at me, eyebrows raised. "You take your boss's dog to the groomer's?"

I flushed. "Once. Helena can be very...persuasive."

"Well, so can I," he countered with a wink. I wasn't in much of a position to argue, so I merely watched as he cajoled Angel into the basin and soothed her with "there, there" while he poured the tomato juice over her silvery blue coat. Angel, of course, made a liar out of me by standing as still as a hairy little statue as he bathed her in the acidic juice and rinsed her with pails of water. She must have been as mesmerized as I was by the sight of Sam in his skivvies. I took advantage of the chance to study him under my tomato-flavored lashes—smooth brown skin, long muscular limbs, a mat of dark chest hair that whorled into his waistband. His dark blond hair had grown since he'd been in New York, and it suited him. But what struck me as most appealing about the man was the quiet confidence with which he handled everything, from a magazine-cover photo shoot to dealing with a skunk attack. Somehow I knew that Sam could handle just about anything that came his way.

The trouble with a man like that was that he didn't need anyone to complete him, ergo the whole no-commitment thing. And I needed to be needed...a little.

He gave Angel a final rub with a towel, then shook his head. "To get rid of the smell altogether, I think we're going to have to give this lady a haircut."

Panic blipped in my chest. "I don't think her mistress would like that."

He shrugged. "You're the one who has to ride home with her."

"On the other hand, a new look for spring never hurt a girl."

His laughter rumbled through the room. "When we get to the pound, someone there can give her a trim. I think I'll reschedule the spaying until tomorrow—she's had enough excitement for one day."

He looked at me for confirmation, and I nodded, secretly relieved to be deferring her discomfort for one more day.

He carried Angel to the bedroom, then closed the door behind her. When he came back alone, he gestured toward the big tub. "Do you mind if I join you?"

My modesty was long gone, and I was relatively sure that nothing naughty was going to happen in this soup. "Be my guest."

I heard him skim off his underwear and made myself not look, although when he climbed into the tub, some things were just hard to miss. He seemed perfectly at ease as he slid into the bath facing me, situating his legs outside of mine, easing down in the water to his shoulders, then dunking under for a few seconds. He lifted his muscular arms and worked the warm tomato juice bath through his hair, then settled back. Beneath the water, our legs brushed, re-igniting those sexual currents. I decided that talking was the best distraction.

"You act as if you've done this before."

"My dogs have scared up a few skunks."

"I feel like an idiot."

He laughed. "Don't. This is the time of year that skunks are nesting, so they're more likely to spray."

"Still, I guess it's pretty clear that I'm out of my element here. I keep messing up." I was miserable, and already wondering how bloated this juice would make me.

Sam shrugged mildly. "Don't worry about it. Nobody expects you to—"

When he stopped, I looked up. "Fit in?"

He hesitated. "I was going to say 'know your way around.'" Then he grinned. "I hope this episode doesn't make it into the article."

"I can virtually guarantee it."

"How's that going?"

"The article? Fine," I lied, and dropped my gaze. The water had separated his chest hair, revealing the pink slash of a vertical incision. He must have noticed me staring.

"My heartbreak scar," he said with nonchalance.

"Are you really okay?" I asked.

"Really," he said, then gestured toward the mountainous view out of the bay window. "Being surrounded by such beauty has a calming effect on a man's life." Then he looked at me and angled his head. "On the other hand, some types of beauty can cause all kinds of problems."

I flushed, knowing I was miles from being beautiful. "Don't tease me."

"I'm not teasing you, I'm flirting with you."

He leaned forward and ran his finger down my nose, coming away with a tomato dreg. "Sorry," he said. "I know that flirting is off-limits."

I looked into his smiling eyes and swallowed hard, and the realization hit me between the shoulder blades—I was in love with this man. Crazily, improbably and unexplainably, I simply wanted to be around him. We had nothing in common, and we lived in different worlds, but his smile made me forget my own name, and his lovemaking made me forget to breathe. The sheer absurdity of it brought moisture to my eyes. The sheer hopelessness of it made me determined to reestablish a professional distance. The sheer irony that I'd reached that conclusion while sharing a bathtub with the man made me contemplate drowning myself on the spot.

"I think this stuff is working," I blurted, then lifted my arm for a sniff. "Now what?"

"You can shower if you like," he said, nodding toward the glass stall.

I hesitated. "I'll be needing clothes."

"I'll find you something to wear." He leaned his head back and closed his eyes—out of courtesy, I realized.

I gingerly pushed myself from the thick bathwater to stand. There simply was no graceful way to get out, and my movements were further impeded by the fear of falling and impaling myself on Sam. As enjoyable as that might be, the act wouldn't exactly lend itself to maintaining a professional distance. I squeezed water-juice from my hair and managed to climb out.

The shower was heavenly. I stood under the spray until the water began to run clear, then I lathered my skin and hair. I had tilted my head to let the spray fall on my face when I heard the shower door open and Sam step in behind me. I tensed as he dropped his mouth to my ear. "My hot water heater isn't that big—we'll have to share."

Warning bells sounded in my head, but he continued good-naturedly. "Don't worry, I'll behave. I wouldn't want you to break out in hives again."

I was glad he couldn't see my face, the way his words and body affected me. I glanced over my shoulder to see he'd turned his magnificent back to mine. He reached for the soap and his behind brushed my hip. "Sorry," he said. I gritted my teeth against the desire stirring in my belly and concentrated on scrubbing my skin. He didn't help matters by whistling a happy little tune under his breath, as if he often took platonic showers with the opposite sex.

"Wash my back?" he asked.

I sighed and turned to accept the washcloth he offered over his shoulder. He braced his hands on his hips and waited. I worked up a lather with the bar of soap we shared, then tiptoed to work the suds into his smooth brown skin. His muscles flexed beneath my fingers and he rolled his neck. "That feels good."

I reached higher, but inadvertently brushed my breasts against his back. He straightened. "That feels good, too."

"Sorry," I said, then covered my zinging breasts with

one arm and continued the slow massage of his back, working lower and lower. The expanse of bare skin coupled with the rhythm and the pressure I applied lulled me into a sexy, drowsy state. The closer I got to the paler skin of his buttocks, the more I thought about what lay on the other side. I had no doubt he sported an enormous erection, and I had to remind myself that I could resist him if for no other reason than because I had a duplicate of said erection in my room. If I simply had to have the man, I could have him later, minus the hives and the emotional fallout.

I abruptly stopped. "All done," I said cheerfully.

"Thanks," he said. "Turn around and I'll do your back."

I started to protest, but his tone was so lighthearted, I didn't want to act as if I thought this was leading somewhere. My back needed to be washed, I reasoned, and he was offering. Besides, I liked having my back washed. Back-washing is an underrated activity. In fact, spas should consider adding back-washing to their menu of services.

I turned around, then held the washcloth over my shoulder. He took the cloth and I braced for his touch. Still, I wasn't prepared for the onslaught of desire when he rubbed the warm suds into my skin, applying just the right amount of pressure with his strong hands. He took his time, massaging every square inch of my shoulders before moving to my shoulder blades and middle back. When the cloth grazed the curve of my lower back, my thighs began to tingle and his rhythm slowed. I closed my eyes and had to bite back a moan of pleasure. My nipples were hardened buds, and I could feel my body readying for him, loosening, moistening.

"All done," he said cheerfully, then handed the washcloth over my shoulder.

I snapped out of my fog and straightened. "Thanks."

"Don't mention it," he said, then opened the shower door, grabbed a towel from a hook and stepped out, wrapping the towel around his waist. "I'll leave some temporary clothes on the bed. Angel and I will meet you at the truck in thirty minutes, okay?"

"Sure," I murmured, feeling cold and deflated by his sudden absence. My body sang with pent-up longing, but I had a handle on my emotions by the time I rinsed and dried off. The near-miss encounter on the heels of the revelation that I was in love with Sam had left me floundering.

When I opened the door to his bedroom, he and Angel were gone, and he'd left a sweat suit and flip-flops on the bed. Everything was too big, but it sufficed. I realized I was making a habit of wearing the man's clothes. On the way out of the cabin, I walked the barking gauntlet of the ugly dogs, then jogged to the clinic as fast as I could to escape the lingering scent of skunk and burnt clothing hanging in the air. I didn't see Sam and presumed he was in the menagerie, where I did not plan to go. I flapped upstairs in my big shoes and rummaged through my rapidly dwindling wardrobe, then donned a long floral skirt and matching jacket, stack-heeled shoes, and a peach-colored Prada blouse. I blew my hair dry, none too pleased that the skunky odor still clung faintly to my thin blond locks, adding insult to injury. I whisked it back in a tortoise headband so it wouldn't be swinging in my face (and under my nose). My pastel striped Kate Spade tote was just the right touch for the season. I realized I wanted to look my best for Sam.

But when I approached the truck where he stood drinking coffee next to Angel's carrier, he surveyed my outfit and shook his head.

"What?" I asked, irritated that I'd taken such care to dress and he obviously didn't appreciate it.

"Get in," he said. "We're going to the pound, and then I'm taking you shopping."

16

THE THOUGHT of going shopping had never failed to cheer me—until now. Admittedly, though, many of my clothes were ruined, and if I had to buy some temporary togs to keep from sacrificing the rest of my wardrobe, then so be it. Maybe Jar Hollow had a Saks outlet tucked away in the trees.

On the way through downtown, Sam was greeted by enthusiastic horns and hand-waving from nearly every vehicle that passed us on the road.

"Nice picture, Doc," a man hooted.

Chickle's marquee and every other changeable sign in town paid homage to Sam:

WE*rE PRoUd of U DR LoNg!
HOmeTown HeRo SANdWich SpeciAL
jAR HolLow SaLUTEs DOC LoNG

"They love you," I murmured.

He laughed and shook his head. "The people here are so good—they love everyone."

I remembered the sneers I'd garnered when I walked out of Chickle's bathroom carrying Angel. "I doubt that," I said.

"Outsiders have to prove themselves," he said. "Me included. Even though I had the confidence of the former vet, it was a while before folks would call on me when they had problems. I think they were afraid I'd laugh at them."

"Laugh at them?"

"Or patronize them."

I bit into my lower lip. Was I a snob—is that why those women had said those things?

When we drove by the Jar Hollow Volunteer Fire Department, a sign had been erected that read Station of Dr. Samuel Long, Hometown Hero. Sam laughed and honked the horn twice. Some men cleaning a fire truck looked up and hollered and waved when they recognized Sam's vehicle.

I got a warm, cozy feeling inside—this was his neighborhood, and it was nice to see people relating to each other. But the episode also reminded me of his fairly dangerous hobby.

"How often do you get called to put out fires?" I asked nervously.

"Not very often, especially since we've had so much rain this year."

"Can you give me an average?" I pressed.

He shrugged. "Maybe once a month. The town is lucky to have a large group of volunteers, so if I'm on an emergency call, I don't feel pressured to respond."

I exhaled. So the chances were good that this week would pass without incident. Of course, whether I could avoid creating further disasters was yet to be seen. Today wasn't going so badly, though—at least the only casualty of the skunk incident was our clothing. I looked heavenward. I could only hope my mohair sweater and Via Spiga loafers were in a better place.

"Where is the pound?" I asked.

"On the other end of town, near the county seat, just a few minutes' ride."

The scenery was lovely. We passed a little park full of swing sets, an elementary school, a drive-in theater and a car wash. Motel, public library, a factory and lumber yard. It was all so alien, yet so familiar, true Americana, quaint things I'd heard about and read about, but had never seen, and wasn't sure I had believed existed. I glanced over at Sam's handsome profile, relaxed but observant, surveying his town. Unbidden, my heart welled up, and I remembered my strategy to interview him for my article when things got touchy.

I dragged out my pad and pen. "How often do you visit the pound?"

"Usually once a week, depending on how busy they are. I do immunizations, and surgeries when they need me, and—"

I looked up. "And?"

"Put the animals down when necessary."

I blinked. "Euthanasia?"

He nodded. "A sad reality of my business. There are way too many unwanted animals in the world."

I put down my pencil and involuntarily reached over to touch his arm. "I'm sorry."

He looked down at my hand, then at me. "It's not your fault, Kenzie."

I withdrew my hand self-consciously. "I mean I'm sorry that you have to take care of ugly things that no one wants to hear about."

His expression was rueful. "I didn't mean to bring you down, but I'd be happy if this article you're writing would help a few animals be adopted."

My heart flinched. Helena viewed my article as a cover, and I viewed it as a career stepping stone. Only Sam had a noble motive.

"Did I say something wrong?" he asked.

"No," I said quickly.

"Good." He flashed his winning smile. "Here we are."

He pulled into the pound and I was instantly cheered by the building's bright yellow and blue paint job. Sam pulled his medical bag from the back, and I picked up Angel's carrier, wrinkling my nose against the odor emanating from her coat.

Sam introduced me to Julie, the volunteer groomer, then left to make his rounds.

"Angel had an encounter with a skunk," I explained to the slim brunette who exuded a serious air. "Dr. Long thought it might be best if she had a haircut."

Julie grimaced at the odor and nodded her agreement.

"Don't worry," I whispered to Angel. "Short hair is in this spring."

Still, I couldn't watch as Julie gave Angel a courtesy "puppy" cut. Afterward, I sucked in a sharp breath. Gone was the long silvery blue hair on her body, left was the tan hair around her face. She looked like a miniature lion. Wearing a pink bow. Helena would have a stroke.

"It'll grow back," Julie assured me. "Arma Chickle told me about you—you're the reporter doing an article on Dr. Long."

"That's right," I said, responding to the woman's friendliness. "It's a follow-up to the hometown-hero issue, it's about his vet practice. Maybe you could give me some insider information."

"About Dr. Long?" The woman smiled. "He's amazing, taking care of his patients and our animals too. I told him he needs to get a life, get married or something."

I laughed along with her. "Has he ever been married?"

The woman shook her head. "But heaven knows, Val Jessum has tried hard enough."

I laughed harder. "Oh?"

She frowned. "You're not going to print that, are you?"

"No," I promised.

"Well, between you and me, Val is kind of high-maintenance, and I think the doc prefers the quiet life."

My laughter petered out. Well, that definitely knocked me out of the running.

"What are you ladies talking about in here?" Sam asked, walking in.

"Nothing," we said in unison, then Julie added, "Except your magazine cover." From behind a counter she produced a copy of *Personality*. "My sister Rachel asked me to get you to sign a copy for her." She handed him a pen. "You're a celebrity. People have been calling here asking about you."

Alarm struck my chest—the tabloid guy? "Who?"

They both looked at me, and I conjured up a smile. "I thought it might make an interesting tidbit for the article."

Julie nodded, then shrugged. "Just local folks, all wishing the doc well."

Sam flushed, but scribbled his name on the cover, then scratched Angel's head. "I'm ready to go," he said to me.

I held up my camera. "Can I get a few pictures?"

"Sure," he said. "I'll give you the nickel tour."

He led me to a room lined with cages. "These are our adoptable pets at the moment. We have a few that are on the mend from various injuries and illnesses in another room."

I saw thankfully that not all of the cages were full, but there were enough dogs and cats on hand to give me pause. I stopped in front of a cage that held a white dog with perky ears who pawed at the cage and barked to get my attention. I snapped a picture. Indeed, all of the animals seemed to realize they were on display and preened for me and Sam when we walked by.

"To be adopted, they have to have a good pet personality," Sam said.

I snapped more pictures. "How long will they stay here?"

"The pound will keep them as long as there's space and food, or six months, whichever comes first."

I balked. "Six months?"

He nodded. "How soon will your magazine run your article?"

I didn't have the heart to tell him that my article wasn't scheduled and if it did run, it probably would be considered filler and given minimal space. "I'll try to get it in ASAP." I put away my camera and walked around cooing to the dogs and cats individually. One black and brown dog was particularly attentive. "Oh, what a pretty girl," I said, clucking to the animal.

"It's a boy," Sam said. "Careful—not all of these animals are used to being around people."

But the dog seemed friendly, sniffing me and making little hoarse barking noises. I straightened and turned to Sam. "What do you mean?"

Too late, I felt wetness seep through my sleeve. I looked back to see Friendly had hiked his leg and taken a pee on my jacket. I jumped back from the cage to the tune of Sam's hearty laughter. "That wasn't funny," I said, peeling off my jacket.

"I tried to warn you," he said. "Are you ready to go shopping now?"

17

"I DON'T believe it," Jacki said sleepily.

"Believe it," I said.

"Kenzie Mansfield went shopping for clothes at a place called Contractor Supply."

"That's right."

"What the heck kind of store is it?"

"They sell building supplies...and clothes."

"What kinds of clothes?"

"Great stuff," I said, rummaging through my finds. "I bought Wrangler jeans like the real cowboys wear, Dickies overalls in a fabulous burnt-orange color, plus unstructured coveralls to die for in black, navy and gray. Just add a Gucci belt, and voila!"

"You'll probably start a new fad when you get back to town."

"And did I mention this place sells Doc Marten boots? I've always wanted a pair, and never had a place to wear them." I picked up the lace-up boots to hug them to my chest. "Now I have them, and they were half of what I would've paid in the city!"

"Good for you. I take it you managed not to kill Sam yesterday?"

"Yes. Although there was a minor incident with a skunk that was sort of my fault."

"You were squirted by a skunk?"

"Yeah. Sam had to burn the clothes we were wearing. My mohair sweater, and my Via Spiga loafers—gone."

"Oh, that's tragic. But doesn't that smell get in your skin and hair?"

I hesitated. "Sam gave me a tomato-juice bath."

"He gave you a *bath?*"

"It wasn't sexy at all." I chewed on a nail. "Although the shower afterward could have gotten a little out of hand."

"You're showering with the man?"

"Just that one time. And nothing happened—he's honoring my request that we keep things professional."

"Did I miss the article on taking professional showers?"

"There's something else, Jacki."

"What?"

"I think I'm in love with him."

"Okay, I'm confused. You slept with him when you didn't know him, and now that you're in love with him, you're *not* sleeping with him?"

"Right."

"No wonder men can't figure us out. Have you told him that you're in love with him?"

"Oh, right, because I haven't done *enough* since I arrived to make a fool out of myself."

"Maybe he has feelings for you, too. He seems attracted to you."

"Jacki, Sam Long lives on a mountain in the middle of nowhere. The attraction is that I'm female."

"Is there a shortage of females in the town?"

"No. But he made a comment that women here want to get married and have kids."

"Oh."

"See? Sam Long has made it very clear that he has no intention of settling down. I should have trusted my allergies and kept my heart under wraps."

"No matter what a man's intentions are, Kenzie, love can still surprise him."

"Okay," I said, waving my arm crazily. "Let's say that by some miracle the handsome, eligible country vet falls madly in love with the city girl with a penchant for disaster and who doesn't even know what gravy is. He can't just pick up his practice and move to the city. And I could never live here!"

"Why not?"

"Well," I said dryly, "the four-hour commute to the magazine twice a day would be a bit taxing, don't you think?"

Jacki sighed. "I guess you're right. And you'll probably feel differently about Sam when you come home and you're not with him every day. Maybe that guy at work who asked you out will help you get over him."

I worked my mouth from side to side. "Maybe." I didn't want to think about Daniel Cruz. "What's going on with you and Ted?"

"Well, I might be reading more into this than I should, but...when I was at Ted's place last night, I found a brochure...on *rings.*"

I blinked. "Engagement rings?"

"Yes!"

My heart raced for her. "He's going to propose!"

"Maybe not—maybe he just got the brochure in the mail. Or maybe one of his friends sent it to him as a joke. Or maybe my mother dropped it off."

"Or maybe he's going to propose!"

"Maybe," Jacki conceded with little lilt in her voice.

"Do you have any big getaways coming up? Special dinners?"

"I'm meeting his folks Friday."

"Well, there you go. He's going to introduce you to his folks, then he's going to propose."

"I don't know. And I don't want to think about it too much—oh, look at the time, I'm going to be late for work. Call me tomorrow?"

"Sure," I said. "Talk to you tomorrow." I hung up the phone and smiled for Jacki—she deserved a great guy in her life. And Ted would be lucky to have her.

I sighed. Love really did make the world go around. We were all in a constant state of loveness—searching for it, participating in it, agonizing over it or recovering from it.

I toyed with the phone cord, then sighed and made the call I'd been dreading.

"*Personality* magazine, Helena Birch speaking."

"Helena, it's Kenzie."

"Kenzie, I just called you and the line was busy! Something's wrong, isn't it? Is it Angel? Dr. Long?"

Apparently I didn't matter. "They're fine."

"I got your message that Dr. Long couldn't do the procedure yesterday—did something come up?"

I took a deep breath. "Angel had a confrontation with a skunk, and although she's fine, she did get sprayed."

Helena gasped. "Is that poisonous?"

"No, it just smells really, really bad. So...we had to give her coat a little trim."

"How much of a trim?"

"She's bald."

Helena wailed. I held the phone away from my ear and Angel lay down, covering her little lion head with her paws.

"Because of all that happened," I said over her wailing, "Sam decided to wait until today to do the procedure."

"Oh, she'll be like all my friends," Helena cried. "Bald

and barren." Then she stopped with a hiccup. "Wait a minute—he can't do the procedure today."

"Why not?"

"Because...something bad is going to happen today."

I squinted. "What are you talking about?"

"I've received...word...that something bad might happen today...where you are."

"Received word?" I touched my forehead. "Can you be more specific?"

"I have my sources."

"On the future?" I silently counted to three. "Helena, are you consulting a psychic?"

Dead silence on the other end confirmed my suspicion.

"That Madame person I took a message from once?"

"She's a genius," Helena said defensively.

I rolled my eyes. "Let me guess—she's the one who warned you about the cover curse?"

"That's right."

"After the first couple of accidents, right?"

"She recognized the pattern."

"She recognized an *opportunity*. Helena, she's a fraud. Accidents happen to people all the time. The chances are good that *anyone* on the front of *any* magazine is going to have a fender-bender or take a fall. Do you realize that your psychic could be the one fostering this curse, maybe even calling the tabloids?"

"Has Dr. Long heard anything?"

"No, but I had to scare off a reporter from the *National Keyhole*."

"Those vermin! Good job, Kenzie. And you might think that Madame Blackworth is a hoax, but talk to me when you're facing menopause—you'll try anything to stay sane."

I bit my tongue to keep from telling her that she wasn't sounding very sane at the moment.

"And I happen to believe in Madame Blackworth's visions. Which is why I want you to promise me you won't let Dr. Long do Angel's procedure today."

I sighed. "Okay, I'll talk to him."

"And keep an extra close eye on the doctor today."

"I will."

"Oh, and you be careful, too. I don't know how I'd ever replace you, Kenzie, if something happened to you."

"Goodbye, Helena," I said, half touched by her concern and half offended by its self-serving angle.

I hung up the phone, looked at Angel and cringed. "Let's find you a pretty sweater to wear today."

I brushed Angel's face and dressed her in a red Polo silk-blend sweater and plaid hair bow. I took a shower and dressed myself in my new five-pocket jeans with double stitched inside seams for extra durability in case I needed to ride or wrangle something. I lamented the fact that my hair still stank, and pulled it back into a ponytail. Then I jammed two halves of a bagel into the toaster and threw in a small load of towels for the sheer pleasure of the convenience. From the window I saw Sam walking toward the clinic, his head bent over a manual.

My heart buoyed. I removed the stuffing from under the door and bounded downstairs to meet him. Angel trotted behind. He walked in the door and grinned when he saw me. "Look at you in your country duds."

I smiled and puffed out my chest. "Ready for duty—what's on the schedule today? Ropin'? Ridin'? Tromping through the mud? Birthin' babies?"

"The high-school mascot has a bad case of lice."

"Oh."

He laughed. "Don't look so deflated—treating lice can be exciting."

"If you say so."

He picked up Angel and scratched her head. "You haven't fed Angel this morning, have you?"

"No."

"Good, because I'd rather she fast before I do the procedure this afternoon. She can have water, though."

My mind raced for a good way to ask him to postpone the procedure. "If you're too busy and need to put it off for another day..."

He shook his head and patted Angel's belly. "No, I'd rather do it today so she can have some recovery time before the car trip home."

I bit into my lower lip. He was already thinking about us leaving.

Suddenly his expression folded into a frown.

"What's wrong?"

He was smoothing his fingers over Angel's exposed belly. "I need to examine her."

Heart thudding, I followed them into an exam room that was furnished with a miniature version of the padded table one would find in a human's examination room. Sam set Angel on the table, then eased her to her side and lifted the sweater to feel up and down her stomach.

"Is something wrong?" I asked.

He looked up. "Nothing that shouldn't resolve itself in a few weeks."

I grabbed the back of a chair. "She only has a few weeks to live?"

"No," he said with a half smile. "She's pregnant."

I gasped. "Pregnant?"

He nodded and pulled down her sweater. "Just barely,

I'd say maybe a couple of weeks along." Angel sat up and barked.

"But Helena never lets her around other dogs—she's terrified she'll get fleas."

His eyebrows rose. "Well, this wasn't immaculate conception. Maybe she got away from Helena in the park—it only takes a few minutes." He grinned. "That part of sex seems to be universal across all male species."

I was too upset to laugh.

"Hey, didn't you say that she disappeared at the groomer's for a while?"

I closed my eyes briefly and nodded. The timing was right. Helena had entrusted me with her prize possession, and I had let her get knocked up.

Angel stood and barked again, this time more frantically—and at the door.

At the same moment, an alarm sounded, and I smelled smoke.

"Something's on fire," Sam said, bolting for the door.

My bagel. My stomach bottomed out as I ran into the hall to see smoke billowing from the upstairs bedroom door.

"Call 911 and get out!" Sam shouted, then grabbed a fire extinguisher from a wall mount in the hall and ran upstairs.

I made the call with shaking hands and a wobbly voice. When I slammed down the phone, I scooted Angel out the front door and started to follow her, then remembered Sam's menagerie.

I glanced up and heard the loud hissing of the fire extinguisher being released. Sam could take care of himself, but the least I could do was try to save his animals from smoke inhalation. I opened the door to the sound of frightened cries and rattling cages. Smoke filtered into the room via the air duct in the ceiling. I unbolted the door in the back of the room that led to the outside and threw it open. It was a little-used back entrance that led almost directly into the woods. I found a rock to hold the door open, then ran back in for any cage I could lift. Again and again, I returned to carry out screeching cats and barking dogs and screaming birds. God help me, I left the rats and the snakes for last. I actually considered just throwing open the aquariums and letting them fend for themselves, but at the last minute, I picked up the rat aquarium and stumbled outside with it.

The snake aquarium took more courage—and strength. I could barely lift it, and being nose to nose with the creatures made me dizzy with fear. Then I spotted a hand dolly in the corner (I had moved enough times to recognize its usefulness). I turned my head, wrapped my arms around the aquarium, and lowered it to the dolly, then dragged it outside to set it next to the other cages lined up on the ground. I heard the distant sound of a fire truck wailing, and only then did I give in to the bone-bending thought that Sam might be in danger.

Because of me.

I heard his voice calling, and I almost ran back inside, until I realized that he was outside, calling *my* name.

"Sam, I'm here!" I ran around to the front where he stood with his hands cupped around his mouth. When he saw me, he briefly closed his eyes in apparent relief, and then jogged toward me.

"Are you okay?" we asked in unison.

"I'm fine," I said, then started blubbering like a big, fat, firebug baby.

He pulled me against his chest. "It's okay. The fire is out, and it looked worse than it was. There wasn't much damage." Then he pulled away and winced. "Except for your clothes."

Clothes, schmothes. I sniffed. "Even my Dolce coat?"

He looked confused, then turned to wave at the fire truck that came into view. He walked over to confer with the men, shaking hands and pointing, obviously diffusing the panic.

I felt a nudge on my leg and looked down to see Angel staring up at me. I leaned over to pick her up, then stroked her head to calm both of us. I watched Sam, horrified to know that my carelessness could have cost him his clinic or his life.

"I'm the curse," I murmured.

18

"YOU COULD have been killed!" Jacki said.

"We all might have been," I said miserably. "I'm a walking weapon."

"It was an accident," she soothed. "I'm sure Sam doesn't blame you."

"He says he doesn't, but what's he going to say? 'Get away from me, you plague?'"

"I actually used that line once on a guy—it really works. Did you lose anything in the fire?"

"All of my clothes."

"No!"

"Yes."

"Even the Dolce coat?"

"Even the Dolce coat."

Jacki moaned. "Well, at least you're safe. Hey, if you set the apartment on fire, where are you sleeping?"

"In Sam's guest room." I laid my head back on the pillows of my new bed. Same woodsy furniture as the rest of the house, but with a camouflage and deer motif. "I offered to get a room in town, but he insisted that I stay here. Besides, it was so late by the time we cleaned up from the fire, I was too exhausted to walk any farther than across the road."

"Well, I have to ask—did the dildo survive?"

"It did," I said. "Do you think there's some kind of message in that?"

"You mean, like 'stop, drop and roll'?"

"No, like I should just be happy with the facsimile."

"Okay, that's just plain creepy. Since when have you been into signs?"

I hesitated, knowing how crazy I was going to sound. But if you couldn't confess crazy things to your friends, that left only Internet chatrooms and daytime talk shows. "I talked to Helena yesterday morning, and she warned me that something bad was going to happen."

"I'm not following."

"Helena consults a psychic, and the lady told her something bad was going to happen here yesterday. I was suspicious because it's the same lady who's pushing the idea of this cover curse, but then again..."

"Kenzie, be serious. Something bad has happened every day you've been there—did she predict those things, too?"

Good point. "You're right. Of course you're right. I think the country air is doing something to my mind."

"Like oxygen overload?"

"Yeah, I need to get back to the smog and exhaust—apparently I operate better on fewer brain cells."

"Are you still planning to come home Sunday?"

"If I live that long."

"Chin up. And call me tomorrow."

I hung up the phone and decided to get the call to Helena over with. If I was lucky, she'd have downed her first cup of coffee. If I was really lucky, she wouldn't pull me through the phone line when I delivered the questionably good news about Angel.

I dialed and waited.

"*Personality* magazine, Helena Birch."

"Helena, it's Kenzie."

"Where have you been? I called and called last night."

"We've been really busy." I cleared my throat. "Helena, there's been a little development with Angel's spaying."

"You didn't allow Dr. Long to perform the procedure yesterday, did you?"

"Um, no—as it turned out, he couldn't have."

"What do you mean?"

"Angel is pregnant."

"What? That's impossible."

I gave a nervous little laugh. "Actually, that's not true. Remember when I took Angel to the groomer's?"

"Yes."

"Well, she sort of got away from me when I took her out of the carrier, and she was lost in the facility for a little while. It was only a few minutes, but Sam says that's long enough to...er—"

"I get the picture," Helena snapped. "What am I supposed to do? I can't raise a litter of puppies in my flat. And God only knows what kind of beast compromised her—the offspring could be huge!"

"We'll find homes for them." I swallowed. "*I'll* find homes for them. In fact, I'll take one." I squinted, trying to remember if my apartment building had a no-pets policy.

"So this was the bad thing that Madame Blackworth predicted," she said.

"It must have been," I said to pacify her. She sounded so forlorn I saw no need to tell her about the fire.

Helena heaved a queenly sigh. "Well, I suppose you can't change destiny. How is that article coming along?"

"Nicely," I lied. Where had my ambition gone? I was blowing it.

"And Dr. Long is well?"

"Yes." So far.

"Hmm, there's my other line, Kenzie, I'm expecting a

call from—well, I'd better go. I'll call later to talk with Angel. I can't believe I'm going to be a grandma!"

I hung up the phone and considered pulling the covers over my head. But I had to face Sam sooner or later, so I dragged myself out of bed and into the shower. Getting dressed was easy—my choices were smoky orange overalls or smoky dark coveralls, all of which had been spared from the fire by virtue of me having taken them into the bathroom to cut off the tags. I chose the overalls and a long-sleeve navy T-shirt from the stack of pullovers that Sam had lent me. Under the T-shirt, however, I was shocked to find my pink Lejaby panties, the ones I'd left for Sam on the bed in the hotel room. Sam must have realized I would need undergarments. Interesting that he'd kept them. I wasn't sure what to make of that, but I was happy to have a clean pair of my own underwear to put on.

My hair—I sniffed and faced the reality: between the skunk and the smoke, it had to go. Where I would find a stylist in Jar Hollow, I didn't know, but I'd have to take my chances when I went into town later to look for underwear and socks. Meanwhile, I skimmed it back into a ponytail.

I dressed Angel in a black chenille sweater and put a festive silver bow in her hair, then I carried her out into the hall lest she be assaulted by Sam's pack of hounds, but all was quiet, except for clinking noises coming from the kitchen, so I set her down. I followed my nose down, then through the den and into the place where I'd doled out our fried chicken dinner just—had it only been four days ago?

Sam stood at the stove with his back to me, wearing low-slung Levi's jeans and a gray T-shirt (Banana Republic, I thought, although I'd have to see it from the front to be sure). He was barefoot and his hair was uncombed and I thought I would die from wanting to touch him. He was nodding his head to the beat of the song on the radio, using a spatula to move sausage around in a cast-iron skillet. He seemed relatively unburdened for someone saddled with me.

My chest tightened and I felt downright miserable in my skin—helpless that I had all these feelings for this man and had made such a mess out of things. I'd given up on the fantasy that Sam would fall in love with me—now I was simply hoping he wouldn't have me incarcerated.

"Good morning," I said.

He turned and flashed a heartbreaking smile. "Good morning. Did you sleep well?"

I nodded, then burst into tears.

He looked alarmed, then abandoned the sausage to steer me into a knotty pine chair. "What's wrong?"

"I almost burned down your clinic," I bawled.

He made soothing noises. "I told you, it was an accident. I have good insurance, and besides, the damage was superficial. And you made sure all the animals were safe." He winked. "Even the snakes. Forget about it, okay? Let's eat, I'm starving."

I hiccuped. "What are we having?"

"Sausage, biscuits and gravy."

I was pining for fruit and cereal, but I wasn't going to argue. He set coffee and a plateful of steaming food in front of me—links of meat and open-faced biscuits smothered with taupe-colored gravy. I sniffed the gravy suspiciously, but my empty stomach overrode my reservations, and I dug in.

Sam was already working on his plate, piled twice as high as mine. He chewed slowly and with obvious enjoyment—a simple act that endeared me to him further.

"This is good," I said, sipping the strong coffee.

He wiped his mouth with a napkin and grinned. "I'm not much of a cook, but I can manage breakfast."

I saw my opportunity. "So...how do you make your gravy?"

He shrugged. "The usual way."

Ah.

"So," he said, "have you talked to your boss about her dog?"

I nodded. "She took it badly, but I promised to take one of the puppies and help find homes for the others."

"Very commendable."

I shrugged. "You inspired me."

His eyebrows rose a fraction. "Thanks. And you inspired me."

My heart bobbed in wonder. "I did?"

"To get organized." He nodded toward the clinic. "The computer and whatever else you ordered were delivered this morning."

"Oh. Well, I'll help you set up everything today."

He made a rueful noise. "It'll have to wait until this afternoon. I need to drive to Syracuse to pick up some meds. And I still have to do that lice treatment. I should be back by noon."

He didn't want me to go.

"Unless you want to go," he added.

Despite Helena's edict for me to shadow him, I wasn't about to force my company on him. Besides, he was probably safer if I *didn't* go. "No, that's okay—I was thinking I'd go into town and run a couple of errands."

He nodded, then resumed eating. So did I, but tension had settled over the room, as thick as gravy. And just as baffling.

"So," he said finally, "do you have enough material for your article?"

He was eager for me to go back to Manhattan. A bite of biscuit stuck in my throat. "Almost."

He took a drink from his coffee cup and seemed to be weighing his words. "I was just wondering, since I won't be spaying Angel, if you were planning to leave earlier than Sunday."

I swallowed. "If you need for me to leave—"

"I don't," he cut in. "That's not what I meant. You're welcome to stay...as long as you need to." He took another drink. "Or want to."

My silly heart might have read something into that last remark except he was looking at his plate, talking to the sausages. He wanted me to leave and was too nice to say so. My appetite vanished, and I was tempted to go pack my empty suitcase and hit the road, cover curse be damned. Angel and I could hide out in my apartment until Sunday—Helena would never know we'd left early.

Unless she called.

I groaned inwardly. No, I had to stick it out, but at least I could help to get his office organized before I left. That might make me feel better about the pretense of my trip, and all the trouble I'd caused since arriving.

"I guess you're missing the city, aren't you?" he asked.

I looked up and nodded. "It's my home. I guess a person misses what's familiar."

He nodded, then glanced at his watch. "I'd better get going if I'm going to make it back at a decent hour." I helped him to clear the table, load the dishwasher, and wipe the wood counters. We moved with few words and in tandem, reaching around each other and picking up where the other person left off. Despite its pioneer appearance, the kitchen was stocked with state-of-the-art appliances, and the wood cabinets featured custom organizers, recycling bins, and storage racks. Perhaps he didn't have Madison Avenue taste, but the man appreciated quality.

"Thanks for the help, partner," he said, then winked and disappeared in the direction of his bedroom.

I stared after him, then took Angel for a walk, hoping the fresh air would help clear my head. But since the air was still tinged with the smell of smoke from my most recent disaster, the walk did little but remind me how much I didn't belong here. And gave me a roaring headache.

Sam came out of the cabin carrying a travel mug as we were stepping upon the porch. "I'll be back in a few hours," he said, then hesitated.

For a few seconds, the scene felt...*domestic* and I had the crazy sensation that he was going to kiss me goodbye. I stepped backward, trouncing on Angel's paw. She yelped and I apologized, then waved at Sam who'd resumed making his way toward the truck. "Be careful." He nodded and I bit back a reminder to wear his seat belt. That was just too telltale—although I did stand there long enough to make sure he buckled himself in. He waved as he pulled away, and when his brake lights disappeared, I was overcome by a pressing sense of loneliness. The trees towered around me. The air echoed with quiet. I wondered if Sam ever felt lonely.

I left Angel in the guest room with food and water and drove the Volvo into town, keeping my eyes peeled for discount stores and hair salons. I pulled over at a dollar store and purchased a package of socks and one of underwear—not French, but sturdy and sufficient to get me through the weekend. I asked the clerk about a hair salon and she directed me to the Cut and Curl within walking distance.

It was a nice day for a walk, and the temperatures had warmed to the mid-sixties, according to the digital marquee on the Peoples' Bank of Jar Hollow. Warm for spring in upstate New York. The street cleaners were out—not the huge raucous machines with spiraling brushes, but two old men with wide push brooms, making their way down the edge between the sidewalk and the street a few feet at a time. From my vantage point I could see the town square and the hustle and bustle there around the fountain. The hair salon was down a shady side street, between a video rental store (free popcorn) and a pizza parlor (free breadsticks). A pink awning marked the door of the salon, and the windows were dotted with taped-up pages from hairstyle books. I squinted—*dated* hair-salon books. I worked my mouth from side to side wondering if I should risk it. Next to the leader of the Free World, the person with the most power was a hairdresser. A hairdresser could make your day, or ruin your year.

Before I could make up my mind, the door opened and a plump woman with a helmet of jet-black curls smiled wide. "Come on in, honey. You look like you could use a friend."

While I was thinking it was a bizarre thing for the woman to say, my feet moved forward and carried me into a long, aromatic beehive of a room full of women having their hair and nails done. Except for the country music playing in the background and the coffee pot in the corner instead of a bottled-water bar, the Cut and Curl could have been a salon in Manhattan.

"Now, what can I do for you, miss?" the woman asked me.

"I need a cut and blow-dry. Do you take walk-ins?"

"Sure do." She consulted a pink appointment book, then patted my arm. "I'll be right back."

I realized that I was being checked out by every woman in the room and tried my best to look unaware. But I found it difficult to maintain my composure when I looked up to see the woman returning with Val Jessum in tow. Val Jessum wearing a pink smock. When she saw me, her step faltered, then she recovered.

The older woman smiled wide. "Val will be glad to take you, Miss—?" She held her pen over the appointment book.

"Mansfield," Val and I said in unison. An awkward stare-down ensued, both of us weighing the implications of her cutting my hair.

"Look," Val said, "if you don't want to do this, I can swap with another stylist."

"No," I said with more aplomb than I felt, then conjured up a smile. "Let's do it."

I followed Val, noticing that many women were reading the copy of *Personality* with Sam on the cover. When we reached Val's station, the cover was taped up in the corner of the mirror. I climbed into the chair as if I were ascending to a guillotine. She and I both knew she could scalp me if she wanted to.

"How long have you been cutting hair?" I asked nervously.

She gave a short laugh. "All of my life." She snapped open a pink plastic cape and fastened it around my neck, a tad too tight. "I left and worked for Sam for a year, then came back." She sighed, as if she regretted the move.

"Sam said the paperwork is killing him, and from the look of his desk, I'd have to agree."

"I thought he would replace me," she said pointedly. "But he hasn't."

Point taken.

She averted her gaze. "Sam and I worked well together."

"He mentioned that." I opted not to mention that he'd

insinuated they had worked together better than they'd played together.

The tight line of her mouth softened and she seemed to be contemplating...*something*—going back to work for Sam? He did appear to be holding a place for her. The fact that she was considering it gave me some idea of what Sam's answer had been to the "Who is she to you?" question.

Val released my hair from the ponytail holder and turned me around to face the mirror. "What kind of cut would you like?"

I was silent for a few seconds, struck by the polar extremes in our reflection—her olive skin and glossy beauty next to my Milk of Magnesia complexion and limp, malodorous hair. "Um...something rather short, I think."

Her lovely brows arched. "Really?"

I lifted a longish lock ruefully. "I had a run-in with a skunk."

She smiled as if she wished she'd seen that. "Can't get the scent out?"

"Not completely." I looked in the mirror and tossed my head, suddenly brave. "And I'm ready for a new look for spring." I swallowed. "What would you suggest?"

She fluffed my hair with both hands, then pulled it back, away from my face. "With your bone structure, you could go really short, like a pixie cut." She wet her lips. "But if you have a special man in your life, you might want to consider that men usually prefer longer hair."

Sam, she was telling me, preferred longer hair.

"Pixie cut it is," I said cheerfully.

I hoped the gleam in her eye was anticipation and not retribution.

19

Two hours later, I pulled into the driveway between Sam's house and clinic and acknowledged a little pang of disappointment that he hadn't yet returned, which scared me because it gave me a taste of how I might feel after I went home.

Disconcerted, I collected Angel from the cabin and paused to finger my close-cropped do. It was reminiscent of Sharon Stone's cut in *The Muse,* except, of course, I was no Sharon Stone. But I had to admit that Val Jessum knew hair. She had even talked me into white highlights to brighten my eyes and my complexion, although at the time I'd wondered if it was only a ploy to keep me there to ask me more questions about city living. Regardless, we had established a rapport, if not of friendship, of mutual respect. Still, when I left she seemed happy to know my visit to Jar Hollow was nearing an end.

And she didn't invite me to come back.

I suspected, as Val apparently did as well, that she'd eventually wear Sam down and they would make a life together in this town.

I pushed aside those thoughts and decided to get a jump on setting up the office equipment. I ventured into the menagerie room to fetch the dolly, and took a few minutes to interact with the scruffy-looking cats and dogs on the mend. I even glanced at the snake aquarium—once. Then I fled.

I hauled in the computer first and had it going within an hour. My dad was a whiz with computers—passing hours tooling around with all the latest software had been a way for us to spend time together and not talk about Mom. I had managed to pick up a few skills along the way. Next I set up the peripheral equipment, and soon the office was buzzing with an electronic whir. I was feeling very pleased with myself when the phone rang. I picked up the receiver.

"Dr. Long's office."

"Kenzie, it's Helena." Her voice vibrated with excitement. "I have great news."

"I can come home?"

"No," she said flatly. "In fact, it's even more important now that you stay."

I frowned. "Why?"

"News of the cover curse hit all the trade magazines this morning."

I frowned harder. "I thought that's what you were trying to prevent."

"I was, but now that the rumor has leaked, our warehouse has been emptied—every copy of every back issue is gone! Subscriptions have skyrocketed, and advertisers are *flooding* in."

My heartbeat spiked. "What does that have to do with me?"

"I suspect that reporters will be contacting Dr. Long, perhaps monitoring him to see if he suffers an injury."

I closed my eyes, knowing how much Sam would *hate* that, would hate me if he suspected I'd come to "supervise" him for the purposes of fending off a silly cover curse. "Again, what does this have to do with me?"

"Well..." Helena's tone descended into the sing-song she adopted when she wanted to persuade, influence, coax and wheedle.

I braced myself.

"Do you think Dr. Long would be open to the idea of *simulating* an injury?"

My jaw dropped, then anger gripped me. "Don't you mean *faking* an injury?"

"We don't have to get wrapped up in semantics."

I set my jaw. "Helena, Sam has integrity—remember the reason you put him on the cover to begin with? He'd never even consider it."

"You sound as if you know him so well—Kenzie, you're the last person I thought would ever mix business and pleasure."

I chose to ignore the barb. "Anyone who has spent ten minutes with Sam Long would know that he'd never go along with something so deceitful."

"It wouldn't be deceitful really."

"How?" I sputtered.

"Madame Blackworth said Dr. Long would definitely incur an injury this week, which is why I sent you up there in the first place. So if you hadn't been looking out for him, he would've been hurt anyway, so why would he mind pretending?"

I touched my forehead in disbelief and spoke slowly. "Because it wouldn't be pretending, it would be *lying*."

"You mean like saying you went there to write an article about him?"

That stung. "I *am* writing an article about Dr. Long. I thought you were giving me an opportunity to advance my career, Helena—was I wrong?"

"No," she said quickly. "I don't want to lose you, Kenzie."

My shoulders relaxed.

"But I do need a teensy favor."

I tensed. "What?"

"Is there some way you could stage a little accident for him to sprain his wrist or maybe break a collarbone?"

My mouth opened and closed, then I gritted my teeth. "*No.* And I can't believe you would suggest such a thing."

Helena made a clucking noise. "Kenzie, I'm trying to protect the jobs of everyone who works for this magazine, including you. You're the only person with whom I could discuss something like this. You have my complete trust...and gratitude."

I was almost nauseous. "Forget it, Helena. I would never knowingly put Sam in danger."

Helena emitted a little laugh. "Well, Kenzie, then I guess there's no reason for you to stay after all."

My heart shivered in disappointment—no reason to stay here...or with the magazine, she seemed to be saying. I tried to maintain a steady voice. "I guess you're right, Helena. I'll leave this afternoon and drop off Angel this evening." I hung up the phone before my voice could break, and then inhaled a long, quivering gulp of air.

I thought I'd known Helena better, but the tough-talking boss I admired would never have suggested something so underhanded. She was eccentric and manipulative, sure. Anal and demanding, okay. Shrewd and controlling, absolutely. Bitchy and—

I frowned and tried to remember what I *liked* about working for Helena Birch.

I heard the door to the clinic open and rose to compose myself. I stepped out in the hall and saw Sam walk through the front door, carrying boxes and whistling under his breath, his brass-colored hair falling into his eyes. He looked up and grinned and my heart splintered, just like the first time I'd seen him, except worse because now I *knew* him. And I was leaving.

"Hey, look at you," he said.

"Look at me?" I asked, walking toward him.

He set down the boxes and reached forward to touch my temple. "Your hair—wow, it's great."

I'd forgotten about my new cut. I touched it, remembering what Val had said about his preferences. He was being nice. My neck started to itch.

His smile faded a bit. "Are you okay?"

Tell him about this curse nonsense. "I'm leaving. Today."

His eyebrows lifted. "Is there an emergency?"

"Sort of," I lied. "At work. Helena called a few minutes ago."

He appeared to be struggling with something to say, probably "yippee."

To change the subject, I pointed in the direction of his office. "I got the computer and the rest of the equipment set up."

"Great, let me take a look."

He followed me to the office, then emitted a low whistle. "Where will I begin?"

"Here," I said, tapping a stack of CDs. "Tutorials to walk you through how to use the computer and all of the software." I cleared my throat. "But you really should consider hiring an office manager again."

He nodded. "I know, and I will."

So Val would have her job back.

He scratched his head and looked all around. "How can I thank you?"

"No need," I assured him, unable to look away from his unfathomable brown eyes. "After all the problems I caused this week, it's the least I can do." The urge to fold myself into him was irresistible. Every muscle in my body strained toward him. *Tell him about the curse.*

"What problems?" he asked, his eyes suddenly turning serious…and hungry.

My knees wobbled, but I managed a laugh. "You're a good sport."

"You're the good sport, agreeing to come here and follow me around for the sake of an article."

The article—my cover. A pang of guilt struck my chest. *Tell him about the curse.* "Sam—"

"This package must be yours," he said, picking up the Neiman Marcus box that had been delivered with the equipment.

"Actually, it's yours." I cleared my throat. "It's...a gift."

He seemed perplexed, but pulled out a pocket knife and slit open one end of the box. He pulled out a Ferragamo box and frowned. "What is it?"

"Open it."

He lifted the lid to reveal the fabulous low-heeled black calfskin boots. He picked one up and stroked the leather. "Nice. But I'm sure these cost a fortune."

"About the same as a custom-made shirt," I murmured. "I guessed at the size."

He looked at the size and nodded, then smiled and looked down at his dust-covered boots. "These are a little more fancy than my steel-toed standbys. Thank you."

I shrugged, pleased. "You're welcome. They'll look great on you." Then before I felt compelled to elaborate, I pointed toward the cabin. "I should go pack."

"I'll come with you," he said, "to see you off."

I walked back through the clinic and outside, my feet heavy as he fell into step beside me. It had turned out to be a beautiful day, sunny with a warm breeze that lifted the tender new leaves on the limbs of the trees. I turned my face up to the sun and inhaled the over-oxygenated air. Now that my leaving was imminent, I had an epiphany that I might miss this place. Barking dogs and all.

Well, maybe not the rats. And the snakes. And the gravy.

Angel trotted along beside us, and Sam picked her up for a ride. "How's the new mama today?"

"Peeing every few minutes," I said.

He nodded. "Sounds about right. Tell your boss this is bound to happen again if she doesn't have her spayed."

"I think she's a believer," I said wryly, already dreading my confrontation with Helena. I pushed aside thoughts of finding another job—I would have plenty of time to ponder my careening career path and other zigzags in my life on the four-hour drive home. *Tell him about the curse.*

We walked into the house and I went to the guest room, pulled out my suitcase, and packed my meager salvaged belongings in record time. When I found the dildo, I hesitated, unsure as to whether having such a blatant reminder of Sam would be a good thing or a bad thing. Still, I packed it. I emerged carrying my suitcase in one hand, Angel's in the other, and set them next to the front door. Now that I was going, I was in a hurry to be gone.

"How do they look?" Sam asked from the doorway of his bedroom, looking down at his feet.

He was wearing the boots, shiny black against the worn hems of his Levi's. And sexy, oh my God. I was sure it was the exact look that Salvatore Ferragamo had had in mind when he designed the boots.

"They look…perfect," I breathed. "How do they feel?"

He took a couple of steps and nodded. "Soft…and good." He looked at me and smiled, then his eyes turned smoky. I knew that look, and I knew I had about three seconds to decide how I wanted this to end.

He held out his hand to me, and I went to him for a long, lingering kiss. *One last time,* I told myself, knowing I was digging myself a bigger emotional hole to crawl into, but throwing caution to the wind. Our lives would probably never intersect again—he knew it too, and the intensity of our desire rivaled that first night, when nothing was at stake.

He broke the kiss and pulled me in the direction of his bedroom, closing the door behind us. He led me to the gigantic log bed and began to undress me. The fasteners on my orange overalls clicked as they fell. He grinned at the sight of my pink panties, and I knew I'd never be able to wear them for anyone else. I pulled at his T-shirt, dragging it over his head, loving the way it mussed his hair. My body was already on fire for him—the sight of his bare shoulders and chest made me want to touch him, breathe him, wrap my arms around him and bring him into my own flesh. When we were both nude, he groaned and eased me back on the cool cotton quilt to cover my body with his. The emotions that welled in me were so strong and so delicious, I had the sense of floating along, with no obstacles to pure joy and ecstasy. I opened my mind to every touch and texture because I wanted to burn the memory of him, the memory of us, into my mind.

He murmured my name against my breasts, then laved each peak with his rough tongue until I cried out. I pushed at his shoulders and rolled on top to straddle him and slow the pace. I kissed his chin, shoulder and stomach. He tensed when he realized my destination, sending a rush of feminine power through my limbs. I admired his erection, remembering the fun we'd had in the hotel bathroom making the dildo cast. Sam was proud of his body and frank with his pleasure, and I was buoyed by his sheer intensity.

I teased the tip of his erection with my tongue before taking as much of him in my mouth as I could. I'd never been into oral sex, but his groans fueled me to try things I'd never done before. I used my lips, tongue, teeth and hands to pleasure him, and the more he responded to my touch, the more I wanted to satisfy him. But a few seconds later, he stopped me with a groan and rolled me underneath him.

His eyes were passion-glazed as he kissed me, rubbing his wet erection against my belly. "You are too much," he murmured. "I can't get enough."

I arched into him. He wrapped his arms around my waist and kissed my stomach, then lowered his head to the juncture of my thighs. I tensed for his touch and when his tongue stroked the center of my desire, I melted into the bed with a sound I'd never made before. He responded to my excitement, pushing his tongue into me over and over. I strained into him, weaving my hands through his thick, silky hair. I could feel my climax coming on fast, so I pulled him up with all the strength I had. His muscles quaked and his erection jutted to its fullest. He did have the presence of mind to find a condom, but when he moved on top of me, he was inside me in a single thrust.

He kissed me and I tasted my passion on his mouth, a heady sensation. We had stoked each other's body to the limit, so within a few seconds, I was pulsing against the length of him in a long, intense orgasm. With one more thrust, he joined me in my white-light eruption. Our moans mingled, then diminished as we recovered. I wanted to lie in his warm embrace for hours, but eventually our breathing returned to normal, and I came slamming back to reality.

Tell him about the curse. "Sam—*oh!*"

A cracking noise sounded and Sam rolled over, taking me with him. After I got my bearings and he pulled away, I turned my head to see that the large-mouthed fish and the board it had been mounted on had fallen, landing where our heads had been.

"Are you okay?" Sam asked, sitting up.

I nodded, trembling. The words that Helena had said raced through my mind. *Madame Blackworth said Dr. Long would definitely incur an injury this week.*

He disappeared into the bathroom to dispose of the condom, and when he came back, I was fastening the straps of my overalls. He lowered a kiss to my temple, then pulled on his own clothes, frowning at the mounted fish. "That thing has been hanging over my bed for years with no incident." He grinned. "Then again, we were really going at it."

I leaned over to lace my Doc Martens, frantic to get out of there before I caused the roof to fall in.

His chuckle sounded across the room. "If I didn't know better, I'd say you were trying to kill me."

I looked up and swallowed, then stood and scratched my itchy arms, already reacting from our encounter. "Ha ha. Listen, I'd better hit the road."

His eyebrows rose, but I race-walked to the door and opened it, practically tripping over Angel in my haste to get to the front door. "Come on, girl, time to go," I said, then picked up our suitcases and nudged open the front door with my foot.

"Kenzie, wait, I'll get those."

"I got it," I said over my shoulder as I trotted down the front porch steps.

He caught up with me. "Where's the fire?"

Tell him about the curse. I stopped and turned. "Sam, I have something to tell you."

"I have something to tell you, too."

I set down the bags. "Okay, you first."

He studied the toes of his new boots for a few seconds, then he looked up and lifted his big shoulders in a shrug. "Why don't you stay?"

"I told you, Sam, I have to get back to work."

He shook his head. "That's not what I meant."

My pulse picked up. "What then?"

His Adam's apple bobbed. "Why don't you stay...for a while?"

My eyes widened. "What do you mean, for a while?"

He looked away, then back to me. "I like you, Kenzie. I like you being here. I...don't want you to go back. Yet."

My heartbeat thudded in my ears. *Yet?* Burgeoning hope was quickly replaced with profound disappointment. I couldn't throw away my life in Manhattan because he *liked* me. *Like* was for sixth graders passing coded notes in class. *Do you like me? Check yes or no.* Val Jessum had put her life on hold waiting for Sam to come around—I wasn't going there. I loved him, but not enough to make up for the fact that he didn't love me. And the fact that he would ask me to upend my life on the chance that things would work between us made things even worse. Sure, I was going to quit my job when I returned, but that was beside the point. Wasn't it?

I blinked away moisture. "I can't possibly stay here, Sam."

He opened his mouth to say something, but the sound of a car pulling into the driveway caught our attention. A boxy sedan pulled in next to my car, then a man got out, mopping his forehead. He waved to us before walking in our direction. "Dr. Samuel Long?"

"Yeah," Sam said, striding forward. "What can I do for you?"

The men met a few feet in front of me, and the visitor extended his hand to Sam. "I'm Terrence Mayo from the *National Keyhole.*"

20

TERRENCE MAYO? My insides went completely still, then launched a revolt. I couldn't decide whether to run or to scream or to throw up, and in what order.

Sam withdrew his hand slowly. "The *National Keyhole*—isn't that a supermarket tabloid?"

The man lifted both hands. "Look, I know you said not to call anymore, but I was hoping you'd talk to me in person."

Sam frowned. "You called here?"

Mayo nodded. "Yeah, I left a couple of messages on Sunday, then I spoke to your secretary."

Sam's frown deepened. "I don't have a secretary."

The guy shrugged. "I spoke to a young lady whom I assumed was your secretary."

They both looked at me, and my face flamed.

Sam straightened. "Kenzie, do you know something about this?"

"Kenzie Mansfield?" Mayo asked. "From *Personality* magazine?"

I nodded, reluctantly.

Sam looked back and forth between us. "Kenzie, what's this all about?"

I closed my eyes briefly to regroup, but no good explanation came to mind.

Mayo emitted a dry laugh. "*Personality* magazine is under a cover curse, Dr. Long, and you're right in the middle of it."

Sam looked completely bewildered.

"Let me explain," I said, my voice sounding stronger than I felt.

He crossed his arms, waiting.

I took a deep breath. "A rumor started that people who had appeared on the cover of our magazine were the victims of freak accidents."

"The accidents actually happened," Mayo cut in, then pulled out a notebook and flipped it open. "Mia Compton, Keith Kellor, Tara Duncan and Jane Suttles appeared on the last four issues, and all of them were injured while their issue was on the stands."

"The injuries were minor," I argued. "And the timing was simply a coincidence."

Sam angled his head at me. "So you knew about this curse?"

"I was aware of the rumor."

"So I talked to you when I called?" Mayo asked.

I nodded.

"Why didn't you tell me about this nonsense?" Sam asked.

I rubbed my mouth with my index finger, trying to signal Sam to be quiet lest he unwittingly give the reporter a story. "Um, maybe you and I should discuss this privately, Dr. Long."

Mayo laughed. "Oh, this is good—the magazine didn't tell you about the curse?"

"He wouldn't have believed it," I cut in. "And by the way, neither do I."

"Really?" Mayo asked. "Then you're not here to keep an eye on Dr. Long?"

I swallowed hard. "No," I squeaked, then cleared my

throat. "I'm here on assignment to do an article on Dr. Long's veterinary practice."

"Right," Mayo said dryly.

"Wait a minute," Sam said, touching my arm. "Kenzie, *were* you sent here to monitor me and report back to your boss?"

I felt like a heel. No, I was something disgusting stuck to the bottom of the heel. "Sam, we really should discuss this privately."

His eyes clouded, and he stepped in to face me and block out Mayo. "All this time I thought you were here because you wanted to be," he said in a low voice. "And instead you were here monitoring my behavior and my calls?"

What could I say? I had done those things. "I'm sorry," I whispered. "It's...complicated."

"So, Dr. Long," Mayo said, "have you had any accidents this week? It'll be a boon to *Personality* magazine if you keep the curse going."

Sam turned around. "Excuse me?"

The reporter looked down at his notebook. "I understand you had a fire here earlier this week."

Sam's jaw went rigid. "That's right."

"Were you injured?"

"No. It was a minor incident."

"Oh." Mayo scribbled. "Any other near-misses since your issue hit the stands Sunday?"

I looked at Sam and I knew he was mentally cataloguing all of my escapades and how he'd had to save my narrow behind more than once. "No," he said carefully, "nothing unusual happened." Then he laughed and gave Mayo a light punch on the shoulder. "Good thing, too, because if it had, I might be tempted to think that Ms. Mansfield had *staged* an accident."

The men shared a good laugh while I shriveled inside. Sam looked at me with one eyebrow raised, then narrowed his eyes slightly for my benefit.

I shook my head and mouthed 'no,' but why would he believe me at this point? I was so mortified, I just wanted to get out of there. I picked up my bags and headed toward my car. "Come on, Angel, let's go home."

"Ms. Mansfield, how about a quote?"

"You couldn't print it," I muttered. When I reached the car, I unlocked the trunk and tossed in the suitcases, then slammed down the lid.

I looked up to see Sam striding toward me, his expression dark. I walked around to the passenger-side door and situated Angel in the seat.

He stopped next to me. "So this was all just a big scam?"

I looked up, but I had to look away again. "No, it wasn't." I walked around the front of the car, opened the driver's-side door and slid onto the warm leather seat.

He followed me. "I don't believe you."

My heart squeezed. "I don't expect you to. Goodbye, Sam."

His mouth tightened—he didn't speak. I closed the door and started the engine, blinking back tears. I was not going to let him see me cry. He knocked on my window, but I refused to look. He was not going to see me cry. I put the car into reverse and sniffed. He was not going to see me cry. I looked over my right shoulder, blinking until I could make out the rear windshield. I hit the gas pedal and we lurched backward.

And over something...solid.

I heard a muffled cry, then jerked around to see Sam bent over, holding his foot.

I'd backed over his foot.

I slammed the car into Park and jumped out. Mayo and I got there at the same time.

"Sam, are you okay?" I asked, gasping for breath. My tire had left a perfect tread print across the soft black calfskin of his Ferragamo boots.

He winced and sucked air through his teeth. "My foot—I think something's broken."

I felt faint. Terrence Mayo whipped out a camera and started snapping away.

21

IT WAS after midnight when the doorman in Helena's building announced me. She buzzed me up and answered the door wearing a marabou-trimmed leopard-print peignoir with matching headband and shoes. She held a drink in her hand and wore no makeup, which startled me for a moment because I'd never seen her other than perfectly coiffed.

"There's my Angel," she said, scooping up her pet. She winced at the dog's haircut, then murmured, "That's all right, we're going to get you a new maternity wardrobe and dress you pretty until it all grows back out." She looked at me and tilted her head. "Kenzie, did you get your hair cut?" Then she scanned my rumpled orange Dickies overalls. "What on earth are you wearing?"

I was bleary eyed and miserable, sleepy and achy, and still itching over my earlier encounter with Sam. I just wanted to go home. I set Angel's suitcase on the floor inside the door. "I'll see you tomorrow, Helena." I would wait to tender my resignation when I was more clear-headed.

"Wait, Kenzie, please come in." Helena dipped her chin. "Please."

I relented and walked in, glancing around her posh condo. Upscale minimalism—collectible furniture, original artwork and orchids. I followed her to a white suede loveseat flanked by two cocoa-colored armless upholstered chairs.

"Please sit," she said, and I chose one of the chairs. "May I offer you something to drink?"

I shook my head, which helped to wake me up.

She arranged herself and Angel on the loveseat and pulled out a cigarette. "Will this bother you?"

"No." I'd never seen Helena smoke, but I wasn't surprised.

She lit the tip and inhaled shallowly, then blew off to the side. "I was glad to hear that Dr. Long is going to be fine."

"Two broken toes isn't exactly fine," I said.

"He's strong, he'll recover."

"I didn't run over his foot on purpose, Helena. I want to be perfectly clear about that."

She smiled. "I know you didn't—you have too much integrity."

I sat stone-still.

She puffed, then said, "Kenzie, I want to apologize for putting you on the spot earlier today. I guess those sales numbers made me heady with the possibilities, but that's no excuse for asking you to compromise your principles."

I was unmoved.

"Also, I suppose I thought you wouldn't mind doing something shady since you were planning to leave the magazine."

I squinted. "You knew I was planning to leave?" That seemed impossible, since I hadn't told anyone.

"I suspected you were interviewing when you started going out to lunch. When you asked to leave early that day, my suspicions grew, and when you came in late the next morning, I knew my days of having an efficient assistant were numbered."

I was trying not to gape. My social life had resumed, and she thought I'd been interviewing?

"And then I walked in on a phone conversation that you cut off." She puffed again. "Plus I know I'm not the easiest person to work for."

She teared up and I shifted on my chair. I'd never seen Helena get emotional about anything.

"But the truth is," she said, her voice trembly, "I've begun to think of you as the daughter I never had, Kenzie." She smiled through the tears. "You're bright and talented and you have quite a future in journalism. I'm not going to ask which competitor has made you an offer—just tell me what I can do to keep you at *Personality*."

I valued my personal integrity, but I recognized a celestial gift when it fell into my lap. On the drive home I'd thought about the article that would probably never see print (especially since I was planning to quit), but I'd fantasized about what angle I could use that would be meaningful to Sam—I owed him that much. And somewhere along the way, I had remembered our conversation about the animals in the pound and had come up with a decent idea.

"I want a staff writing position," I announced. "And my own column. Pet Personality—we can feature celebrity pets and new products, plus encourage pet adoption."

Helena drew on her cigarette thoughtfully, then smiled. "Like I said, Kenzie, you're bright. I think it's a wonderful idea and will be a great addition to the magazine."

Happiness swelled in my chest, but I schooled my face into a stoic expression. "Plus I want a more flexible schedule—three days in the office, two days telecommuting."

Helena hesitated, then nodded. "Our other writers have expressed an interest in telecommuting—I'm sure we can make that work."

I stood and extended my hand. "Deal?"

Helena shook my hand, then stood and gave me a brief hug. "Why don't you take tomorrow off and I'll see you Monday?"

I nodded, relieved to know I could at least sleep in.

At the door, Helena said, "Kenzie, there's one more thing."

I chastised myself for believing that things had worked out and waited for the bomb to drop.

"I know you don't believe in Madame Blackworth's visions, but she said something I thought you should know."

"What?" I asked warily.

"She..." Helena took a deeper drag on the cigarette. "After she spoke with you on the phone, she said she began to get visions about you."

I waited.

Helena shifted. "She said your mother was looking out for you, and that a great love was in your future."

I blinked back unexpected emotion, then conjured up a smile. "Thanks, Helena. I'm not sure I believe her, but those are both wonderful thoughts. Goodnight."

Adrenaline kept me awake on the drive to my apartment, but when I saw my own bed—empty and likely to remain that way—I collapsed into it and gave in to all the pent-up emotion of the week. I loved Sam and now I'd lost him.

22

By the time Monday rolled around, my pillow was a sodden mess, but I had consoled myself that Sam finding out about the stupid curse hadn't changed anything really. From the beginning, the feelings between us had been lopsided—after all, when he'd returned home from Manhattan, he'd called April, not me. He had fallen in *like* with me only after I'd gone to stay with him. And upon hindsight, his request for me to stay there probably had more to do with my computer skills than my emotional appeal.

Somehow I managed to fall back into my weekday morning schedule—grabbing a cup of coffee from Starbucks on the way to work, and arriving at the Woolworth Building early enough to snatch a doughnut from the break room.

On the way out of the break room, I ran into Daniel Cruz.

"Hello," he said with a smile.

"Hi."

"You're back."

I nodded.

"Your hair looks nice."

"Thanks."

"I saw the story about you and the veterinarian."

I managed a flat smile and kept nodding. The cover curse had been picked up by the media and was now up for debate—the mystical camp believed that Sam being hurt was destiny, the cynical camp was convinced I'd run over his foot on purpose to extend the curse.

"So, how about catching that movie this weekend?" he asked.

He was a perfectly nice, perfectly nice-looking man who was interested in spending time with me. It was a shame, because most women would find Daniel extremely appealing, and I didn't. Ironically, the overused line was really true this time—it wasn't him, it was me. It wouldn't be fair to use Daniel as a distraction while Sam was still so fresh in my mind and so deep in my heart. I smiled. "I need a few days to catch up—can I have a rain check?"

"Sure," he said, although the interest drained out of his eyes. "I'll see you later."

I trudged toward my office telling myself that I'd done the right thing for both of us. When I saw the stack of work on my desk, I almost buckled, but told myself that tackling work was the best way to keep my mind occupied. Helena called a staff meeting midmorning and announced my position change and my column idea. April shot daggers at me, but I couldn't even work up enough sentiment to gloat—I had retreated into a sort of haze, moving and responding automatically until I could rebound emotionally from the previous week.

I arrived back at my office to the tune of my phone ringing—a single tone that signaled an external call. My pulse raced, thinking it probably wasn't one of the girls since we'd spent most of the weekend together and I was sure they were thoroughly sick of my whining.

I snatched up the receiver, trying to quell the hope that Sam would be calling.

"Kenzie Mansfield."

"Hi, sweetheart."

I smiled. "Hi, Dad."

"I was calling to see if we could have lunch tomorrow."

I brightened. "Tomorrow? That would be great."

"Actually, I wanted to see what you thought about me staying for a couple of days."

My spirits soared. "Even better."

"Good." He cleared his throat and said, "I was thinking maybe we could visit your mother's grave."

I blinked. To my knowledge, my father had not returned to my mother's grave since the funeral—surely this was a healthy signal. "Um, sure, Dad. I'd like that."

"Good. I miss you, sweetheart. I'll call you tomorrow when I get into town. I'm going to take you shopping and buy you something obscenely expensive for your birthday."

I grinned. "And I'll let you. But really, the lilies were enough."

There was dead silence on the other end of the line. "I wish I could take credit for flowers, sweetheart, but I didn't send any."

"Vanessa probably sent them," I said with a laugh.

He made a rueful noise. "No, Vanessa said she wasn't covering for me anymore." He laughed. "You must have a secret admirer."

I frowned, but thought Dad was probably mistaken about Vanessa. Still, after I hung up, I dug the florist's envelope from my desk drawer and removed the card. Happy Belated Birthday! it still said. Then I turned over the card and gasped. Fondly, Sam.

Then I began to do what every woman does: dissect the gesture for what it might have meant, could have meant, should have meant. Apparently he *had* given me a second thought after he'd returned to Jar Hollow.

A theory popped into my head and I picked up the phone to call April.

"Hello?"

"April, this is Kenzie."

"Yeah, what's up?"

I frowned at her dismissive tone. "When Sam Long called you—"

"Yes," she broke in. "Yes, Kenzie, he was calling about you." She sighed. "He asked for your work address and asked me to recommend a florist, but then I'm sure he told you that while you were staying there. Happy?"

"Yes," I murmured.

"Good." Then she slammed down the phone.

My heart fluttered—this changed everything. Then I sighed—this changed nothing.

My phone rang, another external call. I snatched it up, daring to hope.

"Kenzie Mansfield."

"Is this a bad time?" Jacki asked.

I was only mildly disappointed. "No, what's up?"

"Okay, first of all, Denise and Cindy forced me to make this call."

I frowned. "Why?"

"Because I didn't want to tell you this while you're pining for Sam, but they told me you'd want to know."

"What?"

"Ted and I are engaged."

I shrieked. "Congratulations! When did this happen?"

"Last night. You know, since the family meeting didn't go as well as I'd hoped, I was starting to have second thoughts, and I figured Ted was, too."

"His mother will come around," I soothed.

"It doesn't matter," she said. "Ted and I love each other and we know there are always going to be obstacles, but we want to be together. That's it."

I sighed happily. "It's great that you can be so clear-headed about how you feel and what you want."

"I can't explain it," Jacki said. "When I look at Ted, everything else just seems to fall away and I just know this is right."

"I'm thrilled for you," I said. "And I'm sorry I've been such a blubberhead about Sam that you were afraid to share your good news. And now on to the important stuff—did he give you a ring?"

"We're going shopping Thursday."

"Then why don't the girls and I meet you at Fitzgerald's Friday for some hardcore diamond ogling?"

She laughed. "I'll see you then."

23

"To Jacki and Ted," I said, holding up my glass of wine.

Denise lifted her glass. "And to the biggest freaking diamond I've ever seen!"

Cindy lifted her glass. "And to true love."

Jacki grinned and we all clinked our glasses. She kept glancing at her left hand, as if she were afraid the enormous square-cut diamond might have disappeared since she'd last looked.

My chest was full of happiness for her, so full I hadn't been able to dwell on the sad state of my own heart, for which I was grateful. I had considered calling Sam a dozen times, and changed my mind just as many times. Even if we somehow managed to get beyond the misunderstandings and my duplicity, there was still the matter of his commitment phobia and our geographical distance and my man allergy. And overcoming those kinds of obstacles required more than...*like.*

But for this evening, I pushed regrets from my mind and dished with the girls about movies and hair and ideas for bridesmaids' dresses.

As we were paying for the check, Denise's attention was drawn to something over my shoulder. "Hey, Kenzie, don't look now, but there's a guy staring at you."

I gave her a dismissive wave. "Forget it—I'm taking a break from men."

She shrugged. "Suit yourself, but he looks pretty determined."

I wasn't even tempted to turn around.

"Oh, here he comes," Jacki said. "Eagle Scout, two o'clock."

My heart blipped at the familiar reference, and despite my best intentions, I turned to look.

Then my heart did a back handspring. *Sam.*

He was walking, or rather *limping,* toward me, wearing jeans and a J. Peterman T-shirt (I knew T-shirts) and a cautious smile.

"I think I'm going to call it a night," Jacki said. "Share a cab, girls?"

In the back of my mind, I registered their leaving, but all of my focus was on Sam and on keeping my emotions in check until I knew why he was there.

"Hi," he said. "I was hoping I'd find you here."

I smiled, positive he could hear my heart slamming against my chest wall. "We were celebrating Jacki's engagement." I decided to get right to the point. "What are you doing here?"

He looked at his hands. "Actually, I brought Val."

My heart plunged. "Val?"

He nodded. "She's been wanting to move to the city for ages."

"Oh." So he'd been doing a favor for Val. I sipped the last of my drink to hide my disappointment.

"And when I told her I was coming to see you, she asked if I'd mind if she followed me."

My hopes lifted again. "You were coming to see me?"

"Yes." He shifted to his bad foot, winced, and shifted back. "The fact is, Kenzie, I don't care why you came to Jar Hollow, just that I was able to spend time with you. I'm sorry for implying that you might have staged some of those accidents—I know you would never do something like that." He smiled. "You once said that a person misses what's familiar, and the truth is...I miss you."

I inhaled sharply. "You miss me?"

His Adam's apple bobbed. "In fact, I love you."

"You *love* me?"

"Yes. I knew as soon as I saw you'd carried out my animal cages to save them from the fire."

"I almost left the snakes," I felt compelled to admit.

"But you didn't." He stepped closer and picked up my hand. "I saw in your electronic organizer that you were going to start looking for a nice guy, and that you made the entry *after* you met me. But I came to see if you have any feelings for me. Good ones, that is."

Astonished, I looked at our hands, palm to palm. "Yes, I have some *good* feelings for you."

He looked immensely relieved, and went into alpha mode, gesturing emphatically. "I've been giving this a lot of thought and you don't have to feel pressured or anything, but I was thinking maybe I could arrange to teach some classes here in the city so I could see you more often, and...and we can just see where this goes." He cleared his throat. "And as far as your allergy to me, well, I'm prepared to take things slowly, so you can build up your immunity."

"Wow, you *have* been giving this some thought."

He blushed. "I can't live without you...partner."

My heart soared, and I blinked back instant tears. When I looked at Sam, everything else fell away, and I just knew it was right, as Jacki had said. He and I belonged together.

"So," he said nervously, "do you think we can give this a go?"

I nodded. "I think we can give this a go."

He reached for me and I looped my arms around his

neck and met him for the sweetest, most joyous kiss imaginable. I pulled back and looked at the love shining in his eyes and I was flooded with the feeling that as Helena's psychic had hinted, my mother was indeed smiling down on us.

Yet I couldn't ignore the issues between us that remained to be resolved. "Sam," I said solemnly, "we do have a few things to clear up before we can move on."

Sam straightened, as if preparing for a litany of emotional debates.

"Exactly what *is* gravy anyway?"

Epilogue

TO HELENA'S consternation and relief, the cover curse ended with Sam, but the magazine had gained enough sales and media attention to leapfrog a couple of competitors. My Pet Personality column was a big, fat hit, expanding to a full page after only a few months. We were flooded with celebrities vying to have their pets featured—plus book interest from two publishers. Best of all, we were credited with boosting pet adoptions all over the country.

Helena and I grew closer, especially after Angel gave birth to her three little mongrels. Luckily they took after their mother and were mostly Yorkie, with a splash of something that put a curl in their long coats. As promised, I took one to live with me, and Jacki took one. April Bromley, who had purported not to be a dog lover but had melted when Helena passed out pictures of the litter, took the remaining pup.

Val Jessum adjusted to city living quite well...with the help of Daniel Cruz.

Thanks to gallons of green tea, or maybe just plain old acclimation, my allergy to Sam improved, then disappeared altogether, although Sam still insisted on performing impromptu examinations under my clothes—just in case the hives had reappeared, he said.

Sam taught me how to make gravy—white, brown and tomato-flavored. (I didn't know there was such a thing.) Oh, and after ten months of living and loving together, he proposed and I accepted. Our bridal registry was at the Jamison Hardware Store in Jar Hollow and Neiman Marcus in Manhattan. Jacki, Denise and Cindy gave me the most splendid bridal shower—with the most special gift.

They had the dildo bronzed.

What happens when a girl finds herself in the *wrong* bed...with the *right* guy?

Find out in:

#866 NAUGHTY BY NATURE by Jule McBride
February 2002

#870 SOMETHING WILD by Toni Blake
March 2002

#874 CARRIED AWAY by Donna Kauffman
April 2002

#878 HER PERFECT STRANGER by Jill Shalvis
May 2002

#882 BARELY MISTAKEN by Jennifer LaBrecque
June 2002

#886 TWO TO TANGLE by Leslie Kelly
July 2002

Midnight mix-ups have never been so much fun!

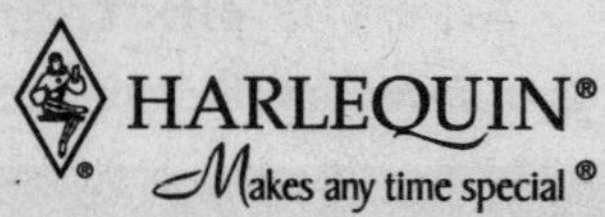

Visit us at www.eHarlequin.com

HTNBN2